MW01181787

Copyright Page

Reid just killed her father. There's no way Evelyn's gonna mate him now… Dammit.

Werewolf Reid Bennett has one goal: investigate the Brookfield clan's Itan. Reports are coming in that the male is abusing his werebears and--even if he's a werewolf--Reid will put a stop to it. Unfortunately, the resolution ends up being permanent and now Reid's the clan's leader.

The only positive about his new situation: curvy werebear Evelyn Archer. She makes his wolf howl and he aches to explore every inch of her lush frame. He's the clan's leader and he knows exactly where he'd like to lead Evelyn—his bedroom.

Evelyn doesn't know what to do with Reid. Sure, he's the sexy wolf her werebear wants to nibble and claim, but she has bigger issues to deal with. Such as the fallout of her father's death… at Reid's claws. Okay, maybe she can take a break for one little lick...

They both have plans for the Brookfield clan… and each other. Except there's a small problem—someone wants them dead. Nothing new for Reid, but a threat against Evelyn is unacceptable. When it comes to Evelyn, he'll break all the rules to keep her safe, including dusting off his homicidal tendencies again.

Chapter One

Reid really wished he had a smoke. Or a drink. Damn, a drink would have been nice. Just a shot to soothe his nerves a little. Unfortunately, his therapist—in another bid to get him to calm down—decided drugs would mask the problem.

Since when did beer and smokes become drugs? It didn't matter. Mainly because his wolf was even more pissed than normal at not having its beer and smokes. How's that, Miss Therapist?

He should take a picture of what happened when he didn't get his "drugs" and text it to her.

Sometimes a patient takes two steps forward and one step back, Mr. Bennett.

A dead body? Huge step back.

Nothing for it, he was gonna have to call it in. The question became, who did he get in touch with first? His therapist since she wanted to be his number one go-to person when he had an "episode" or his boss Terrence, the Southeast werebear Itan?

Considering Reid was a wolf and he'd killed a bear…

With a sigh, he dug in his pocket and tugged his phone free. He sought out Terrence's number and then tapped the contact. It rang once… twice… and then the male answered.

"What happened now?" Terrence growled.

"Aren't you merry fucking sunshine this morning?" he couldn't help goading the bear. The Southeast Itan may have helped him out of a tough spot—taken him in when the Southeast Alpha kicked his ass to the curb—but that didn't mean he couldn't give the male shit. Pack or not, Reid was still as alpha as they came. Submitting to a bear just wasn't in his wolf's skillset.

Killing though… He nudged the bloody body with the toe of his boot.

"Reid, who died?"

Take out one bear before sunrise and everybody thought he was some sociopathic murderer.

All right, it'd been a pack, one whole pack, that day, but the assholes screwed with his family—and then covered it up. Wolf didn't particularly care for that and showed 'em.

Maybe he was a sociopathic murderer. But if he was, was this murder really on him? Terrence knew he was a fucked up piece of work. If anything, the death of this bear was on his shoulders, not Reid's.

Now he was thinking like his half-sister and the woman's best friend.

"Reid," the other male snapped.

"What?" he snarled.

"You called me. What do you want?"

Right. Wolf hated being challenged. Sorta why he was in this situation.

"You sent me here to Brookfield."

"And?"

"Just laying out the facts, boss man."

"Reid…"

"Wolf don't like your tone," he growled.

"Your wolf and I came to an agreement, and it'll get over it until we meet again. What. The. Fuck?"

"Kiss your kids with that mouth?" Now he grinned because giving him shit about cursing around his half-grown children was fun as hell.

"Reid." The tone, the way the r rolled off his tongue and ended in that rough d told him he should quit playing with the bear.

"We got a problem."

"What kind of problem?"

Reid stared down at the male before him. He took in the guy's size, ignoring the deep wounds that cut to the bone as well as the shallow cuts that marred his chest. Those were from when he'd just been playing with the bear, showing him he shouldn't mess with his wolf. Pure fact, at the best of times his beast didn't like being challenged. Without beer and smokes? Like was no longer in his vocabulary. Loathed though… That was a little more accurate.

The wolf did some good work on the man's legs. One long stripe from hip to ankle. Nice and clean. Part of him—way down deep and almost forgotten—experienced a twinge of regret. Not a big portion, but there was something.

Then he remembered who threw the first punch. And the second. Then the third strike was a kick.

Reid warned him good and hard before he retaliated.

Making a big mistake here. Stop now and walk away. Keep this up and I'll own all your shit in the next fifteen minutes.

It'd taken eight.

Eight minutes of fangs, claws, and blood and now Reid Bennett—sociopathic murderous werewolf—stood over a dead body.

"Problem's about six-two, six-three. Between two twenty, two hundred fifty pounds. Hazy on that since there's a shitton of blood on the ground." But that sounded about right. Head wounds bled like a bitch. Thinking about bleeding had him looking over his own body. He had a nice set of claw marks down his chest, but it was just a flesh wound. His wolf took care of in no time. His biggest concern was his shirt. He liked that shirt.

Terrence sighed and Reid imagined the male was sitting at his desk, leaning back in his chair, and pinching the bridge of his nose as he stared at the ceiling. He'd seen the position often enough. Mainly when Reid had done something. "Tell me it isn't the Itan."

"It ain't the Itan," he immediately replied. How should he know? It wasn't like he checked the bear's ID before the dick took a swing at him.

"Do you even know who it is?"

"No." He shrugged. Wolf didn't care who stepped up. Just that it wouldn't back down.

"Can you please verify his identity for me?" The words were hissed into the phone and he knew Terrence was gritting his teeth.

Reid rolled his eyes and bent down, shoving his hand into one pocket and then the others until he found what he was looking for. "I have Patrick Archer. Huh, guess it is the Itan."

Well, that sucked.

"Fuck me."

"Not my type, but thanks, boss man." He grinned.

"You're not taking this seriously," the bear snapped.

Reid tossed the wallet onto the male and then clenched is free hand into a tight fist. "When I found him trying to rape a twelve-year-old bear, I took it very seriously. When I stopped him and that asshole tried to take my head, I took it very seriously. Calling you, looking at that piece of shit and wishing he was alive so I could kill him all over again… Yeah, my wolf is feeling fucking serious."

"Dammit." Terrence bit off the word. "You were supposed to observe and report."

"I'm not just observing shit if I see something like that happening. It won't fly with me." Ever. He had too much history with that kind of bullshit. He might understand males going at each other but a male trying to rape a female. He was a twisted asshole, but not so twisted he could watch that happening.

"Fuck. Fuck, fuck, fuck." He ended with a roar and Reid knew Terrence's anger had shifted from what Reid did to why he acted like he had. "Who else knows?"

"Probably the kid I sent packing, holding her shirt together and bleeding from a few holes in her side. Girl fought and she was still wearing her shorts when she left. Tough little bitch." He had to appreciate a girl with that kind of strength. Not a single tear on her cheeks. A hell of a lot of appreciation in her eyes though. He wondered how long he had before she spoke to someone and they came looking for him. "Need to tell me what to do here, boss."

"Fuck." Terrence sighed. "I'll make some calls, but until further notice, you're the Itan in that town. You may even end up there permanently," that last bit was mumbled but he heard it anyway.

"You're kidding me."

"I told you I'd shove a clan at you at some point."

Sure, it was a constant threat, but come on. "But I'm a wolf."

"You just had to kill him. You couldn't have held him for me? I'm not that far away, Reid."

Reid's shoulders rippled, the wolf really hated being questioned and Terrence was doing a lot of questioning. His fingers tingled with the need to bear his claws while his gums ached with his slowly emerging fangs. He'd managed to keep his ass in check while he fought the animal, only busting them out when it looked like there was no other end to their fight. "No, I couldn't have held him for you. The asshole was gonna die, Terrence. My hand or yours, he was a dead bear walking."

"And now you're the proud owner of a clan. How's that feel?"

Chapter Two

Human blood tasted different from a deer. Definitely from rabbit or squirrel, too. Though, in truth, Evelyn didn't have much of a comparison to go on since the liquid filling her mouth was her own. She'd never experienced the coppery flavors flowing over her tongue, and she had to admit, she didn't care for the experience.

That didn't stop it from coming though. Especially not when the fist that caused her to bleed collided with her cheek, yet again. The resounding crack echoed off the basement walls and the red liquid flew past her lips in a wide arc that created a gruesome painting on the smooth tile. She went ahead and spit what remained, clearing out her mouth so the blood didn't dribble down her chin. Kinda hard to be a bad ass while she salivated all over herself.

Mouth empty once more, she slowly tore her attention from the fluid sliding down the drains and back to that violence-loving male. And then she smiled widely, stretching her cheeks despite the swelling that marred her vision and the gash on her cheekbone. Wearing rings while beating the shit outta someone wasn't smart. Not when he wasn't trying to kill her. He just wanted the truth.

"Who," he panted with the exertion. Apparently kicking her ass—even while she was tied up and unable to move—was difficult. "Who did you talk to?"

Evelyn licked her lower lip, testing the split while trying to ascertain her injuries. "No one, Uncle."

Uncle. One of three and then there was dear old Dad, but he'd disappeared about an hour ago. Or more. Possibly less. It was hard to tell in the wet room. Steel walls, tiled floor, drains every six feet. It was the first time she'd been down there, but not the first she'd heard of it. She saw two males dragged through the clan den and down the stairs in the first few days of her arrival, but she'd kept her mouth shut. Bears—shifters in general—were violent creatures that required a strict sense of order to stave off chaos. She was new to the clan, her father's bastard half-shifter daughter, what did she know?

Her mouth remained shut and she didn't ask questions. Didn't mean she didn't listen though.

Then she wondered why the hell her grandmother's will ordered her back to his den. And because it'd been in the will, she'd had no choice but to go. She no longer belonged to her grandmother's clan. She was part of Brookfield now and clan law required she present herself to her new Itan. Do not pass go, do not avoid returning to her hometown.

Which was how she found herself in a screwed up, perverted clan that lived and breathed death and rape. Even now, half-dead from being beaten for days—four? Five?—she wanted to vomit.

Those two males? Killed for objecting to sharing their mates with her father—the Brookfield Itan.

The women ended up in his hands anyway. His and her uncle's.

"Stupid bitch, you made a call. Simone heard you," her Uncle Daniel hissed. "Who was it?"

Simone. God, she prayed her little sister got away. The moment she'd met her dad's eyes and then his Enforcer's—none other than Uncle Daniel—she'd known there was trouble. She'd spun and shoved, pushing Simone down the front steps, with a shouted run!

The battle afterward was brutal and punishing, Evelyn fighting not just for herself, but trying to delay their pursuit of her half-sister. And she didn't blame Simone for ratting her out. Life in Patrick Archer's home was kill or be killed. Simone didn't want to end up dead… or the next taken to the basement. She wouldn't put it past her father or uncles, either.

"I didn't talk to anyone."

The next strike was a backhand. At least he went for her other cheek that time.

"Liar."

Yeah, she was, but she didn't think he could scent it beneath the blood.

Daniel balled his fist, pulled back his arm, and she braced herself for the next punch.

"Brother," the single word was murmured, but Daniel froze. Hell, her third uncle stilled as well. That was what happened when Uncle Ezekiel spoke. "My turn."

Her mind flipped through the Brookfield inner-circle. Patrick Archer, Itan. Daniel Archer, Brookfield Enforcer. Sean Archer, Healer. Ezekiel Archer, Keeper… and so much more. Had he not been so batshit crazy, he would be the Itan. But he wasn't and his grip on reality waned with each day. Only Patrick could keep him in line. Barely.

Ezekiel's turn? She was screwed. Literally and figuratively. She just wondered when he'd rape her. Dead or alive.

It hadn't been the first day. Or the second. Or the third…

The truth settled into her bones. After being tortured for days, she finally accepted that help wasn't coming. She'd risked it all, her own life as well as Simone's, with that rash call and for what?

Hope died, but pride at even trying continued to fill her.

It'd had to be her, she'd had to be the one to risk everything to save the clan. They'd suffered years of abuse, years of being constantly battered and threatened by the inner-circle, and they were all… broken. Shells of who they could be. Why hadn't they reached out?

Fear. Death—murder—was a powerful motivator.

The only person Evelyn loved—her grandmother—was gone, but her teachings lived on in Evelyn's heart. She should never—ever—allow those weaker than her to suffer if something could be done about it.

So she'd taken that phone number scribbled hastily on a tiny slip of paper by her ex-Itan. His handwriting was hardly legible, the numbers smooshed together to form the method of her salvation. After fighting to figure out what they said, she'd made the call.

The voice on the voice mail was soothing, a soft timbre that gave off a feeling of comfort and then those words…

"You do not have to bear your pain alone. Leave your name, number, and a brief message and assistance will be sent to you."

Bear your pain… Sent to you…

She'd left a message, short and concise and… begging for help.

Staring into her uncle's eyes, she realized help wasn't coming. Or, at least, she wouldn't live long enough to see her clan freed from the Archer males.

Evelyn played with Daniel, taunting and teasing him, when he came down to toy with her. In between those lovely visits, she suffered through her Uncle Sean's treatments. She wasn't sure why he bothered stitching her together just so Daniel could tear her apart again.

Ezekiel's steps were slow and measured, the homicidal gleam in his eyes frightening and she fought back the tiny shudder of fear that overtook her.

But he caught it. Caught it and smiled wide, exposing his pale fangs. The tips were sharpened, a hint longer than a natural human's, and she knew his beast lurked just beneath his skin.

"I like you afraid, Evelyn," he murmured, voice low but it felt as if he roared through the room.

That was her fear talking and she hated it. Instead of saying anything, unwilling to reveal the depths of her terror, she gathered saliva and blood in her mouth and spat at him. The red scattered over his face, marring his tanned skin with the liquid.

Instead of striking her, he smiled even wider, his eyes turning the full black of his bear. And with him so close, invading her space, she caught something rise above the coppery tang of her own blood.

Desire.

A quick glance at the juncture of his thighs revealed he was hard.

Maybe if she taunted him, he'd end it before he violated her. She hoped.

"Blood do it for you, Zeke?"

"Your blood." He ran a finger along his jaw, gathering droplets as he went, and then he slipped it into his mouth. He moaned with the movement, pure pleasure coating his features. "Delicious."

"You're one sick fuck. You know that, right?"

He shrugged. As if being a perverted psycho was normal.

In Brookfield's world, it probably was. Which was… sad.

"Who did you speak with, little bear?" He made a fist and then uncurled his fingers one by one. As each finger lifted, a claw formed, a gentle fan revealing his deadly intent. Then the process was reversed, those claws receding as he reformed that fist.

One, two, three, four, five. Fist.

Five, four, three, two, one. Paw.

One, two, three, four, five. Fist.

Five, four, three, two, one. Paw.

It was hypnotizing in a bizarre, macabre way. The transitions were fluid and graceful, almost beautiful in their simplicity.

"I didn't talk to anyone." She wouldn't tell them they asked the wrong question. They'd figure it out soon enough. Or they wouldn't and would only realize their mistake when help came. Or didn't.

The claws weren't surprising, the deep furrows cutting a fearsome path across her face. They dug into her flesh, scraping against her bones as they slipped easily through her features. They'd kept her injuries restrained to punches and slaps. Apparently that was done.

She didn't have the strength to spit anymore. Not as the pain thumped through her body to the beat of her heart. The agony was so bright it blinded her with its intensity, vision flashing white with each pummeling wave.

"Who did you speak with?" His voice was calm, as if he hadn't just clawed half her face. When some of the pain ebbed, she squinted through her swollen eyes and noted his features were calm as well.

He didn't care. Not a bit. She wasn't sure why she was surprised.

"No... one..." she rasped, and she realized her words were hardly audible. O... un...

He must have understood because his hand returned. He kept the claws restrained though. He simply dug those fingers into the wounds he'd created, sinking into her flesh and pulling.

And she screamed. God, did she scream. The loudest yet, it bounced off the walls, tearing from her very soul, releasing into the world with a whip fast rush.

"Try. Again."

Try again? He wanted her to speak? She couldn't even breathe. Pain did that. It stole every hint of strength from a body until only it existed. It crept into every muscle and bone, replacing the very blood in her veins with its power.

But she didn't have to. Not when the pounding of a fist against steel resonated from the other side of the room and ended Ezekiel's torture. His hand loosened and he slowly pulled it free of her flesh before finally turning toward the room's only door.

"Open it," he snapped. Uncle Daniel was quick to respond. Daniel may be the clan's Enforcer, but Ezekiel held the power when her father wasn't around, through brute strength and evil.

The door swung open to reveal one of the weaker bears, the male cowering and hating what was to come.

The brothers had no problem killing the messenger.

"What?" Ezekiel growled.

"We have a problem." The way the male trembled, the slump of his shoulders, told her he had very bad news. But his cowering posture wasn't the only thing that let a tendril of hope slink past the pain. No, it was two new scents that the bear brought with him—death… and her father's blood.

Despite her pain, despite the agony that stole the very oxygen from her lungs and the new rush of blood that came with the movement, Evelyn smiled. "Zeke," she waited for the deadly male to look at her with those midnight eyes. "Go fuck yourself."

Chapter Three

Reid hadn't meant to tail the girl, but it was kinda hard not to. Wolf liked a good chase and the kid had to have some idea about why he'd been called. So that's what he did. Oh, she was quiet as hell and nearly lost him when she took to the trees, but he was a better tracker than she was an escape artist. Bears—human or on four feet—may be able to climb and make it from tree to tree, but they always forgot about the leaves. Leaves that their bodies brushed and then fell to the ground as they made their run for freedom.

He wasn't sure who she'd been running from to learn her tricks, but he didn't have to see her to chase her.

Hell, he knew who'd been on her tail. Patrick Archer. How many times did he corner the kid? Didn't seem like the first, but he was thrilled it'd be the last.

Reid kept his wolf near the edge of his control, animal hunting for her scent while his human eyes scanned the terrain. The farther they moved from Patrick—and civilization—the more the geography changed. They headed up a mountain, dirt giving way to rocks, and the trees slowly thinned. They didn't disappear, they hadn't traveled that far, but their closeness lessened.

She was running out of forest, which meant she'd have to make her stand soon. And he wanted to catch her before she shifted. He could keep her from changing, but if she got there before he did… he hated forcing a shifter back into their skin. But he'd do it if necessary. Bear or wolf, lion or hyena, Reid could control 'em all. Except Terrence. The bastard was strong as hell.

A tree fifty feet ahead of him rustled and he flicked his gaze at the surrounding vegetation. Her path to freedom had ended, which meant Reid broke into a run, watching the girl's descent. She climbed down as if she was part monkey and jumped away from the trunk when she still hovered fifteen feet from the forest floor.

And that's when he pounced, tackling her before the first bone snapped or the first nail darkened to a black claw. He kept a tight hold on her squirming body, wrapping around her as they rolled and keeping her from harm. It was things like that that made Terrence tell Reid he was a study in contradictions.

Reid told Terrence to go screw himself.

The girl struggled harder, kicking her legs and digging her slowly sharpening nails into his arms. He wasn't gonna tell her he liked the pain. It told him he was alive, he was breathing, he wasn't six feet under, and he still had another day of fighting in front of him.

"Let me go," she growled and yanked against him.

"No." He didn't bother ordering her to quit fighting. It'd be a waste of breath. He'd just let her tire herself out so he remained in place; flat on his back, the girl's back against his front and arms tight with one leg capturing her two.

Who was the monkey now?

Didn't matter. She'd relax in three... two... and—a few more growls and scratches coupled with an attempt at a head butt. He'd teach her how to do it properly later. Then... one.

A low huff was followed by a soft sob and her scent told him she was done. The fight she'd clung to during her race to freedom had finally given out, which meant she was ready to listen.

And tell him what he needed to know.

"You done?" He had to get her used to his voice.

The girl whimpered and remained silent.

"Here's what's gonna happen, kid. I'll let you go. What you'll do is get to your feet and try to run. I say try because I'm faster, I'm stronger, and if I hafta, I'll get my wolf to keep your ass still. Hate doing it, but I will. You get me? So, since I know what you have planned and you know what I'll do, how about we skip that shit and you take it easy?" He kept his normal snarl outta the words, but she stiffened and trembled anyway. Fuck. He wasn't cut out for kid shit. Give him an adult to maim and torture and he was fine.

Dammit, Terrence was right. He shouldn't have killed Patrick. He hated when that happened.

The kid nodded.

"All right. Here we go." He did as he said, but he gave her a little nudge, forcing her to roll right while he headed left and snapped into a crouch with ease. He kept his gaze on her while also remaining conscious of their surroundings. He didn't bring out his claws—yet—and stayed low. "You good, kid?"

She trembled, those eyes wide, but nodded. He took in her appearance head to toe. Clothes were a little torn and more than one gaping hole marred the fabric. Patrick or the trees? A couple of scratches bled and stained her pale skin, but all in all, she was breathing and she wasn't raped.

A motherfucking win.

"Good," he grunted and slowly rose, still staring at the world around them. "Now, tell me who you are and what the hell is going on here."

She swallowed hard, meeting his gaze for a split second before lowering it to the ground with a low whimper. Dammit. He hated that shit from women and kids. He used to not care, but then his first therapist got into his head about blah, blah, bullshit. But something musta sunk in because now his wolf hated it.

Pussy beast.

"Si-Si-Simone."

When she didn't say much else, he nudged her along. "Uh-huh."

"He-he-he…"

Reid stepped forward and he had to give Simone some credit, she didn't budge. He bent down enough to enter her vision. "Spit it out, kid. He tried to rape you. I got that. But what is going on around here? Someone called the Southeast Itan. You know who? You know why?"

Simone swallowed hard and her attention flicked to his face before turning to the ground once more. "E-E-Evelyn. She called and said our Itan... It's always been this way, but... She... She attacked them and told me to run."

All right. At least he had a name. "Look, kid. That asshole back there was your Itan. I killed him. Now this shit storm is mine. Where can I find her and whoever else I'm gonna need to kill to get things settled. Because I gotta tell ya, I don't really feel like being the Itan here. I wanna kill and go. You help me with that?"

She swallowed hard once more, attention still on the rocks at her feet. "My-my—" he was really getting tired of her stutter. "His brothers. The inner-circle and they-they-they have her."

Brothers. What was it about bears that had them giving birth to four kids to make up inner-circles? He was glad he was a wolf. They just fought shit out and it was done. This leadership by birth crap was bullshit. "All right. Might as well get this over with. Where can I find 'em?"

"They're at the clan den." At least the stuttering was gone. "In the wet room with Evelyn."

A wolf had to appreciate a place like that to kill assholes. Hopefully they'd still be down there and make cleanup easy. "Anyone other than them gonna give me shit about Patrick?"

Simone shook her head. "They're the strongest. You have to watch out for Eze—"

Reid waved her off. "I got it kid."

He'd read the files when Terrence put him on the road. He probably should have paid more attention to the pictures though. He rubbed his jaw, thinking about Patrick's broken body. Yeah, a little more focus wouldn't have been a bad thing. Like, actually looking at 'em at all. Eh, nothing to do about it now. The wolf was anxious to get back to the hunt and tear into a few bears that had Simone trembling and this chick Evelyn calling in the cavalry.

"Where am I headed?"

The girl peeked at him once more. "Over the ridge, three miles."

He grunted in acknowledgment. "There a reason you're hiding this close to the den even though the Itan tried to rape you? I'm guessing it ain't the first time, either. Man was a little unhinged and there was no missing he wanted you." At her head shake, confirming his accusation, he clenched his jaw. Wolf really begged to lose his shit. Soon. "I can scent that you've been here a while. Why's that?"

"They're strong, but they don't know how to track or hunt."

"You do?"

She nodded.

"And if the Itan and inner-circle didn't teach you shit, who did?"

She licked her lips. "Jack. In town."

"Reason you ain't staying with Jack, then?" Kid shouldn't be living alone on the side of a mountain.

"The Itan would have found me. My father would have killed Jack."

"Who's your daddy?"

"Patrick," she raised her head, any hint of fear and trembling gone as hate took their place. "Patrick Archer."

Well, fuck him sideways. He sighed. "All right then. Lemme go kill your uncles real quick and I'll come back for you."

"You say it like it's easy."

Reid smirked, anticipation thrumming through his veins. "That's 'cause it is, kid. That's 'cause it is."

And fun as hell, too.

* * *

The younger male shifted from foot to foot, unease crowding the aromas filling the air. Evelyn realized her bear was filtering through the scent of her own blood and fighting to focus on the others. Daniel's anger, Sean's worry, Ezekiel's joy. They all swirled through the air to join the kid's.

"What?" Her uncle snapped at the young male once again.

"We were out patrolling and found Patrick—"

Zeke's fist shot out and slammed against the side of the kid's head.

"Sorry, sorry," the male immediately apologized. "We found Itan Archer in the forest. Someone killed him. A wolf."

Her uncle vibrated with rage, the joy vanishing beneath his rush of anger, and she smiled. The other two were surprised, Daniel furious while Sean was more thankful than anything. But Evelyn? She was overjoyed.

Zeke lifted his arm once more, but the bear didn't run. He should, everyone knew her uncle's strength, but he also knew running was pointless. Hell, once they were caught, the pain tended to be ten times worse than what they would have felt had they stayed put.

Now, with her father gone—who cared who killed him—the Southeast Itan would have to be called. Salvation came with his death. Knowing safety would come soon, their savior close, she couldn't allow another bear to be harmed. Not while she could save him. Her uncles couldn't put her six feet under with the Southeast Itan's impending arrival. She could pull shit she wouldn't have dreamed of.

Evelyn gathered spit in her mouth, sucking on her cuts and collecting as much as she could.

Then she let it fly. She spat it at her uncle, across the six feet that separated her from the door. It struck his back, splattering his shirt and hitting his neck as well. The red painted him, and the collision had him freezing in place.

Once more she drew attention to herself to save another and once again she wouldn't regret it.

Zeke slowly turned and glared at her, flashing his rapidly changing fangs. His jaw distorted, breaking, and quickly reshaping to form his snout. "You cunt."

She let her crazed emotions free and her mind shatter just enough for her suppressed bear to climb forward. She could imagine what she looked like; carved face, blood coated, midnight eyes that glowed even in the bright light...

"Touchy, touchy." She pouted. "I like talking dirty as much as the next girl, but coming from you, that doesn't make me hot. You get off on the blood, the screams." She flicked her gaze to his groin and smiled wider even as she fought the urge to vomit. A rapid look at the trembling male and she had his attention. She shifted her gaze from his and to the right, encouraging the messenger to flee. "I'm just giving you what you want. You have the blood." She smirked. "And I'll scream for you."

A new scent crept into her a split second before the source stepped into view. He didn't sneak or creep, he merely filled the doorway as if he had every right to be in the house.

A wolf in the bears' den.

A wolf with blood staining his clothing and obvious claw marks marring the fabric.

"Baby, you won't be the one screaming," the newcomer drawled and that touched something inside her.

That had her bear suddenly paying close attention to the world around her. It'd distanced itself from her human consciousness, separating as the pain grew to consume every inch of her body. It had the animal willing to endure the agony for the chance to get a better look at the wolf who'd managed to take down the clan's Itan.

Zeke spun. "Who the—"

And that was it. That was all her uncle said before a single strike sent him reeling. She got a good look at Zeke's face as he turned. Blood flowed freely from the new wounds. Four deep furrows from forehead to chin destroyed the left half of his face and he kept going until he collapsed at Evelyn's feet.

One strike sent her insane uncle to his knees.

Just for giggles—because she'd lost her mind at some point—she spat on him again.

Ezekiel pushed to his feet, a snarl on his lips as he glared at her. Red liquid bathed his left eye, but it was still effective.

Too bad the pain coursing through her and the elation at the wolf's presence made her not give a damn.

She only prayed he'd deliver and make them all scream. And cry. And beg. And sob. And...

Zeke attacked with a roar in one blurring move, but the wolf... didn't budge. Hell, he didn't even brace himself to take her uncle's weight. He simply held fast and pushed back. It was enough to send Zeke stumbling once more. The retreat gave the stranger room to step forward, and in two strides, he stood before Evelyn. One booted foot to the seat of her chair sent her skidding over the tile until she struck the far wall. The legs screeched against the tile, metal leaving deep gouges in her trail as she was shoved to safety.

Then it got real.

Evelyn's move was the catalyst, permission to her uncles to begin the fight in earnest. Which they did.

Ezekiel was first, his fury tangible and obvious as he pounced. Daniel and Sean were right behind him. All three attacked at once, fangs bared, claws out as they went after the wolf.

The wolf smiled widely at their approach. And it was that hint of crazy, the sparkle and tinge of enjoyment that graced his lips that made her breath catch. She knew insane. She saw it every day across the breakfast table and experienced it herself when the world crowded around her.

This... was worse. It was more. It was harsher. It was unforgiving. It was...

When the wolf caught all three of them in one fluid move, she realized it was beautiful. It was elegant in its simplicity, the careful duck and graceful arc of his arm with his claws bared. She watched as if he moved in slow motion, the male taking his time and making the most of each strike.

And he smiled. It wasn't in grim satisfaction, but pure joy. Then there was the laugh, and the elation in the sound was unmistakable. The edge on it, the balanced beast and human, frightened her as much as it intrigued her. She refused to acknowledge that she liked it. That she was attracted to the male.

Because that was fucked up. Not just because she was in no shape to get frisky but also because she was pretty sure she watched him nearly gut Uncle Daniel. Bile gathered in her throat at the sight, rising from her stomach, and she fought to push it down. They'd destroyed her, hadn't they? They'd hurt, maimed, and killed so many. She shouldn't feel bad or be disgusted by what she saw.

Not when Daniel landed a punch.

Or Sean got in a good swipe.

Or Ezekiel…

Where the hell did Ezekiel go?

The knot of bodies continued their battle, males performing a bloody dance that had to end at some point. They would die—the wolf or her uncles. That was the only outcome, there was no other. Then they turned, the brawling mass shifting from one side of the room to the other as the stranger chased Daniel while he planted a boot in Sean's middle. Daniel crawled toward the single door, a wide stripe of blood staining the pale tile. And while Sean struggled to his feet, the wolf pounced onto Daniel's back. Two hands, a yank, and then it was over; her uncle's lifeless body collapsing to the ground in a dead heap.

Which left Sean. Sean the reluctant participant, Sean the uncle who always patched up others, Sean… who'd never attempted to get anyone in the clan help. She'd made a call—one—and she'd been beaten. But at least she'd tried.

So when the wolf flicked his attention to her as if to ask permission, she said the only two words in her mind. "Do it."

He did. One more throw, one more punch, one more pounce, and one more wrench of a head.

Now she was left with a panting male standing above two dead bodies, his chest heaving with the exertion, but she noticed something else about him. Not a hint of fur peppered his skin and his eyes remained human. Yes, the strength of his animal was present, but the beast's presence was nowhere to be seen.

The wolf let her uncle's body fall to the ground, his head banging against the tile, and he stepped over Daniel.

His steps didn't falter, each one firm as he strode through the puddles of blood—hers and theirs. When he was close enough, he crouched and reached for her bindings. A quick tug had her arms free and then the restraints at her ankles disappeared. He didn't attempt to touch her or help her from the seat. He simply remained in place, brown eyes focused on her.

"E-E—" she licked her lips and winced with the sting. "Ezekiel got away."

He shrugged. "I'll hunt him in a little bit."

She nodded and then voiced the only question banging through her head. One both her human and bear wanted the answer to. "Who are you?"

"Your new Itan."

"You're a wolf," she rasped.

"Ain't that the truth, but Terrence doesn't give a fuck." He shrugged.

"Terrence?" She swallowed hard. The Southeast Itan was named Terrence. He couldn't mean...

"Yup, the bear needs someone to do his dirty work, and baby," he licked his lips, gathering a few droplets of the blood that lingered there. "I love dirty."

Chapter Four

Women. God. Damned. Women.

Screw that. It was one. One, battered, bloodied, curvy, and sexy as hell even when she looked like she was gonna die, female.

The werebear currently scaring the shit outta him also made him want to commit murder. The need to kill something didn't really bother him. The scaring him though… that wasn't cool. He was Reid Bennett, alpha asshole, badass motherfucker, and homicidal wolf. Nothing scared him.

Except the aforementioned battered, not-quite-so-bloodied, curvy, sexy, half-dead woman.

"What the fuck?"

He didn't have to yell. Not when all conversation quieted at his appearance. Everyone froze in place, wide eyes trained one him as he slowly strolled into the room. He pretended he wasn't covered in dirt and grime, blood drying on his skin and soaked into his clothes. Mud crumbled and littered the ground with every step, leaving a line of filth in his wake. Memories of his mother scolding him for trailing grass and crap into the house reared up and he kicked it back down. He didn't have time for a painful walk down memory lane. He still needed an explanation for the shit in front of him.

Mainly a—was that wound seeping blood?—half-dead Evelyn puttering around the kitchen.

She hadn't looked at him yet, continuing to pad from the stove to the granite-topped island and back again, attention on her task. The only sounds in the room came from her, from the soft shuffle of her feet and the occasional hitch in her breathing. It was enough to nearly send him over the edge. His wolf wanted out to rip them into small pieces for letting her do anything but lay in bed and recover.

"I said," his tone remained harsh, but he kept his voice even. Evelyn was busy pulling a pan from the oven and he didn't want to startle her. "What the ever-loving fuck?"

The large male sitting at the breakfast bar carefully turned on his stool, identity gradually revealed with the careful movement. At least the idiot had enough self-preservation to move slowly. His wolf was ready to tear into anyone who drew his attention. It was angry—furious—over Evelyn's continued work. She was baking, that much was obvious, but not a single man in the den should have let her on her feet. Sure, her inner-bear worked to repair the damage—many of her cuts and scrapes were nothing more than harsh red lines of skin—but she wasn't healed by any stretch of the imagination.

Eventually the man faced him entirely and Reid glared. Fisting his hands, he stomped toward the male and he resisted the urge to punch the werebear in the face. Barely. "Asher, what are you doing here?" Reid's palms stung as his claws pricked his skin. "What the hell—"

The clatter of metal on stone cut him off and his attention immediately snapped to Evelyn. "Woman!"

He abandoned Asher. He'd kick the bastard bear's ass later. All the way back to his hometown in Grayslake. For now, he was forgotten and Reid focused on Evelyn, on the pan that'd clattered to the counter and sent cookies scattering over the island. "What the fuck?"

She reached for them, thin shirt pulling taut on her back and droplets of blood slowly staining the fabric. He wrapped his fingers around her wrist and stopped her from snatching the obviously oven-hot dessert. "What are you doing?"

She gasped and tugged, attempting to break free. Her wide-eyed gaze collided with his, her light brown irises flickering midnight as her bear rushed forward and then retreated just as quickly.

"Reid," she sighed and relaxed, no longer fighting him.

And that was all it took to calm his wolf; the soft whisper of his name from her bow-shaped lips. The animal damn near purred in response to her voice, her nearness. Pussy beast.

It didn't disagree.

"Evie," he murmured and softened his voice. "What are you doing? I left you in bed with Simone to recover. My orders were clear. Lock the doors and heal. No one in or out until I got back."

He'd managed to take that time before he rushed out the door after Ezekiel. Spared fifteen minutes to shout for Simone, get Evie settled and under the care of her younger sister before he bolted. It'd been a dick move—the woman needed him—but his wolf overwhelmed him with the need for vengeance, for blood. His beast was consumed with a killing rage and it demanded he chase Zeke.

He'd done the best he could at the time. Secured her, ensured she was healing, and then hunted the last bastard who'd hurt her.

Ezekiel disappeared after crossing the stream that bordered the northern edge of the clan lands using the water to mask his retreat. He would have continued if he had others with him, but alone, there was no way he could find the new trail and follow it to the end.

So he'd returned… to this.

"Evelyn," she whispered back and she trembled, her free hand coming to delicately rest atop his. Her fingers drew circles on his flesh, drawing his attention down, and making their differences abundantly clear. That one snapshot was enough to tell him Evie— the name Evelyn was too pretentious—wasn't his concern.

Even if the wolf craved her. Even if the wolf howled for her. Even if the wolf…

She was pureness and light, her hands unblemished by destruction and death. Reid was… everything she wasn't.

Damn. For the first time since Terrence took Reid into the clan, he wished his therapy would have been more successful. But he was still the wolf who liked to kill things, who liked to play with his prey before destroying it beyond recognition.

"Evie, why aren't you resting? I made sure you had protein in the fridge. Did Simone not stick around?"

"I-I-I—" Simone's stutters came from the opposite side of the room, the young girl curled in on herself as she sat on the counter. It was then he noticed the room's setup and location of others.

And the way she was positioned between them all. The males in the space were at the breakfast bar, each of them known to him—obviously ordered to leave Grayslake and come to Brookfield. Then there was Evie in the center, cooking of all things, while Simone huddled and hid while remaining in sight.

"Reid…" Asher growled. As if Reid would hurt a child. He'd killed Patrick for—

"It's fine," he snapped at the bear and then focused on the girl. "You're fine, Simone. Your sister here is another story."

The kid nibbled her lower lip. "She didn't… She only…"

"We're good," he assured her and wondered where all this kindness was coming from.

"Uh, Reid?"

The urge to rip Asher's head off rushed forward and he realized he still had those homicidal urges. Good. At least he hadn't been pussy whipped.

Yet, the wolf assured him. Yet.

"Shut up, Ash. I'm talking to Evie and Simone." Not them or the women. Not strangers, not random bears he was sent to protect. Somehow, as he'd chased Ezekiel across clan lands, they'd become more. The wolf was forced to breathe their scent with each pounding step, draw it in with every gust of wind, and fill him as the blood dried on his skin.

His.

Wolf wanted 'em. Wolf was taking 'em.

"Now, is one of you going to explain why Evie is baking when she should be resting?" Simone remained quiet so he focused on the woman. "Evie?"

"Evelyn."

"You can keep saying that but it ain't changing what I call you. Now answer the question."

It was Evie's turn to nibble her lip and he reached for her with his free hand to cup her cheek. The tension in the room ratcheted up, the males at his back tensing. The change in the air, the slight shifting of scents told him more than one bears' fur slid from their pores. Two years as part of the clans, working for Terrence, and still they didn't trust him. Then he remembered he'd never given them a reason to. Focusing on the woman before him, he used his thumb to gently tug the small bit of flesh from between her teeth. It was freed and he brushed the redness, soothing whatever ache remained.

"Evie?" he murmured. She still hadn't answered him. If one of these assholes rolled her outta bed because they were hungry, he'd...

"Your friends came—"

"They're not my friends."

Asher gasped. "I'm hurt."

They both ignored the dumb bear.

"—and they were waiting outside the house. Ash knocked—"

"His name's Asher," he snapped. He didn't want her using cute nicknames with other males or getting close to any other shifter. It pissed off his wolf.

"I told her to call me Ash. We're friends, too." He could hear the smile in Asher's voice.

He wondered if the bear had a death wish.

"—yelled through the door that they were here to help you and then Terrence called and... I didn't think it was him at first. Why would the Southeast Itan call here?"

"Because I told him I'd resolved the problem."

He ignored Asher's snort and his mumbled, "If you call murdering everyone resolved."

Reid continued. "And that we needed to come up with a plan to assist the clan in recovering from the twisted shit your father and uncles had going on."

Her eyes flickered to her bear's and back again. "How do you know it was twisted?"

"Evie," he gentled his voice. "They tied you to a chair and nearly destroyed you. I caught Patrick trying to harm your sister." Simone whimpered and he was glad he hadn't voiced the truth. "There was no way the males treated the clan like they deserved. And the torture wasn't limited to you two. And if it continued as long as I suspect, your clan needs bears strong enough to protect all of you."

"I'm sure there are some good bears in the clan already."

"I'm sure there are," he quickly agreed. "But until we know who to trust, I need men like these at my back."

"Aw, he likes us," Asher murmured.

Reid was gonna gut the werebear and put his head on a pike.

"None of what you told me explains why you're in here baking cookies," he kept his tone soft. The strain in her eyes was unmistakable, the stress of the day and pain etched into every line of her face.

"He said I could trust the males he sent—that I should let his bears into the den—but I don't know them. If I allowed strangers in the house, I refused to hide in a room with one door and one window. I wasn't going to let Simone and me be that vulnerable."

It made his dick hard that she thought of safety and escape.

"And…"

"And they grilled steaks for us and I refuse to sit on my hands."

Reid lowered his head, bringing their faces closer. He breathed deeply, sorting through the scents surrounding them, finding hers. It was sweet and light, goodness tinged with an edge of bad. That was the part of her that goaded the three males in the basement and attacked while sending her sister running. It was the part he wanted to roll in.

"And? That's not it. Why are you up and baking?" Her attention flicked to the small group of males as a tendril of unease unfolded. "Don't look at them, look at me. No matter what you say, I have you. They let you do this. How bad do I need to hurt them for letting a wounded female wander around the kitchen when she should be in bed?"

His bed.

She licked her lips, the small move heading straight to his dick. He pushed the feelings down, shoving them aside when all he wanted was to throw her on the counter and sink into her wet heat.

Evie's words were rushed. "The kitchen has the highest number of weapons, the easiest method of retreat, and the best defensible position in the den."

"That," Asher drawled, "is hot."

Reid wondered how angry Terrence would be if he killed the bear.

Chapter Five

Evelyn—not Evie no matter how many times Reid called her that—wasn't sure what was going on. Like, at all.

Grayslake bears moved in and out of the den, carrying boxes, moving furniture, and sometimes removing pieces out of the house entirely. All under Reid's close scrutiny.

The place was torn down to its bones, a new long wooden table now situated in the dining room and a few couches in the living room. Asher scented the bedrooms, Reid on his heels, and together they hauled away different pieces. The only spaces relatively untouched were her and Simone's rooms.

Now, he leaned against the archway to the kitchen, the ever-present Asher at his side. It was the first time she'd found him anything close to alone and she padded toward him, intent on finding out what the males were doing.

"Reid?"

His amber gaze swung to her. "You're supposed to be in bed. I put you there—again. I expect you to stay there," he snapped.

That had her glaring. "I'm a grown woman."

"Who had half her face ripped off."

Evelyn turned her head, thankful her long hair fell forward to cover her damaged cheek. The pain no longer plagued her and she forgot about the wounds, the way they'd left her skin scarred. "That's not the point."

"Dammit, Evie," he growled and all movement around them ceased, each male freezing in place.

She wasn't sure why they were so afraid of Reid. She'd seen evil, stared it in the eye and begged for whatever they had to give. Because hurting her meant they weren't hunting for Simone. "I just wanted to know what was going on. Why everything is being taken away. You're destroying my home."

Another growl and it seemed as if the whole room held its breath while Evelyn... didn't. She knew she angered him, but the urge to tremble and quake didn't assault her. "I'm cleaning my home."

She wasn't going to address ownership. Not while he was snarling.

"And I'm removing anything that's tainted by fear and hate."

She frowned and turned her head enough to expose her eyes and meet his stare. "How can you—"

Reid's arm shot out, hand brushing her hair away. The tension in the room ratcheted higher, consuming her in the males' unease, but she only had eyes for Reid. His callused fingers, bare of the blood and dirt that'd covered him hours ago, cupped her cheek. His thumb stroked her chin and then he shifted his hold until he was able to encourage her to look at him fully.

"Because I've caused it often enough. I'm familiar with every scent, every emotion, of every action, of every breath someone takes and each twitch of their muscles." He caressed her lower lip, much like he had in the kitchen, and it had the same effect as before. Her breath hitched, heart stuttering, and a tiny flare of desire snaked into her blood. Could he scent it? The flash of his eyes told her he could. "So when I say they're tainted, they are. They were used to cause fear or pain. They're infused with those scents and I refuse to live with them in my home."

The ability to discern the smells surprised her a little, but the last two words astounded her. She wasn't sure why, really. He'd taken the place of the Itan. Even if he was a wolf, he was the leader of the clan. But still... "Your home?"

What would happen to her? To Simone?

"I misspoke," he whispered against her mouth and she suddenly realized how close they'd become. She should back away, put space between them and shake her attraction off. "Our home. Me, you, and Simone. This place is ours."

"I don't... I..." She'd been so strong for so long. She'd had a purpose for years. Survive as a half-werebear with her grandmother's clan. Work through medical school. Endure her father's clan and uncles' treatment. Now... "I don't know what's going on here, Reid. I'm lost."

"And I found you. You're not lost anymore." His kiss was gentle and she didn't have the strength to retreat. Hell, she didn't want to pull away. Despite the emotional destruction and the physical pain still pummeling her, she wanted to stay close to him—to the male who'd killed without remorse. "You're mine."

"The clan is yours."

"Evie," his gaze was unwavering. "The clan became mine the minute I tore your father's heart from his chest."

"That was some twisted shit," Asher murmured and Evelyn had to agree. As much as her father deserved to die, that seemed a bit... excessive.

Reid spoke as if he hadn't heard Asher, but she didn't doubt the words reached the wolf. He seemed to know everything about, well, everything. "But you became mine the second you told me to snap your uncle's neck."

She wasn't proud of that moment, the two words that left her mouth as she stared at the man responsible for the deep gouge in her calf. "But..."

"But nothing. It's done. I don't expect you to accept me. We don't know each other and I'm not sure if you scent me the way I smell you because you're a half shifter, but you're mine." His lips were soft, another careful brush of moist skin on skin and she couldn't help but lean into him. Her curves easily molded to the hard planes of his body and she sighed into his mouth. He retreated just enough to speak against her lips. "I'm gonna do my best to be patient, but I'm not leaving. I fought for the clan and I'm keeping it. I'm keeping you."

"Reid, you can't just…"

A harsh cough startled her, reminding her they stood in the kitchen in front of everyone. She jerked in his arms, intent on getting away, when Reid's growl had her freezing in place.

"Asher, so help me God, I will rip off your head and shove it up your ass," he snarled and Evelyn followed the direction of Reid's gaze.

"Noted, but," Asher tilted his head to the side with a quick jerk, "just telling you we've got company."

Evelyn twisted farther, turning in Reid's arms as she focused on the doorway—on the handful of bears crowding the porch. One woman stepped forward, hand resting on the curve of her swelling stomach. Katherine. One of her father and uncle's regular visitors.

"Katherine?" Evelyn's low whisper was echoed by Asher, but she ignored him. "What's going on?"

The woman took a hesitant step forward. "Simone called."

Reid's hold loosened, but he didn't release her. In all honesty, she didn't want him to. Not when his last words continued to whisper through her mind. I'm keeping you.

"She said… Is it true?" Katherine's gaze flicked from Evelyn's to Reid's and back again. "Are they… Simone said we had a new Itan. That it was safe to… Is it?"

Evelyn tilted her head back to meet Reid's stare and when he spoke, it wasn't to the pregnant woman, but her. "I ripped Patrick Archer's heart from his chest, I tore Daniel Archer's throat from his body, and I snapped Sean Archer's neck. We'll burn them to ash and celebrate their deaths." She trembled and Reid's hold tightened, squeezing her just shy of painful as if he was afraid she'd run from him.

"And…" Katherine's fingers tightened on her stomach and there was no missing the fine tremble that overtook her small frame. "And the other."

And Ezekiel? That was the woman's true question. Yes, Katherine was a regular visitor, but she was Zeke's favorite. Everything inside Evelyn said the baby Katherine carried belonged to her uncle.

"As soon as I find Ezekiel, he will suffer the same fate. I lost him at the creek, but I will find him." Reid's gaze remained on Evelyn as he gave Katherine that deadly promise.

"Good." Evelyn placed a hand on his chest, memorizing the beat of his heart and the flavors of his scent as they surrounded her, filled her. "I'm glad."

Glad her father was dead and her family along with him. She had Simone—and Reid?—and that would be enough.

A sob tore through the room, snaring their attention once more. Katherine slumped, fingers pressed to her lips as tears cascaded down her face. Asher was the closest and he darted forward, catching her before she tumbled to the ground. Her eyes were closed, as yet another cry erupted from her throat, but one message was easily heard. "Thank you," she whispered. "Thank you, thank you, thank…" she hiccupped and then Simone was there, her small body nudging Asher away and the two clung to each other.

Evelyn had known them only a few weeks—a short time compared to the other women in the clan—and she worried what other atrocities they'd endured.

When those thick arms tightened around her, his face buried in her hair, she slowly realized they'd discover the answer… together. Whether she liked it or not, apparently.

Chapter Six

Reid managed to keep his hands to himself after that embrace near the kitchen. He watched Evie fuss over Katherine and a few other females who'd crept into the house over the last several hours. It wasn't until he got a good look at them all, the way they shied from the half dozen Grayslake bears and clung to each other, that he realized the size of his problem.

This wasn't a matter of a few assholes getting off on pain. He'd met plenty of those, killed more than a few. This was… Goddamn. It was something. Something Terrence hadn't warned him about. He kept his gaze trained on the whispering women, their voices low but still discernible. They were worried, petrified, about him, his men, and what was to become of the clan.

Apparently killing their nightmares didn't calm 'em any. What did a guy have to do to get a little appreciation?

The AC kicked on, blowing a new wave of cool air through the room and as one, the women swung their attention to him. He got five frightened looks, along with a single dose of curiosity from Evie. Well, at least she wasn't afraid of him.

With a sigh, he ran a hand through his hair and sought out Asher with his gaze. The male was a pain in the ass, but dependable and strong as hell. If he could manage to sew the bear's mouth shut long enough, he'd be a perfect second. Which was probably why Terrence sent him along on the trip.

Asher came toward him the minute their eyes locked. His steps were soft and slow, careful in an attempt to not frighten the women. He should just tell the male not to bother. They were gonna be afraid. Not much to be done for it.

"Itan?" Asher murmured.

"I need to make a call. None of the local bears have made an appearance, but if they do, they don't come inside. Tell 'em an official announcement will happen in the next few days. For now, they have a new Itan. No other women in the house unless Simone gives the all-clear."

"Not Evie?" Asher frowned, brows furrowed.

"Evelyn," he snapped. If anyone was going to annoy the shit out of Evie for the nickname it was gonna be him. "And she's new to the clan. Kids…" His gut clenched, memories striking him in the heart. "Kids hear everything, and remember it all. Use her knowledge."

"True enough," the bear nodded. "True enough."

With a grunt of agreement, he left the small group in the living room and was damn thankful there was a local furniture store. He'd sent out men to replace nearly everything, and if females continued to show up, they'd need a place for everyone to sit. He wasn't too sure about the males he'd eventually encounter, but he'd worry about those fights when the time came. For now, he had other worries.

Reid fished out his phone and ran his thumb across the screen. He had fifty-four missed calls. Huh. Less than he thought. Even as he stared at the phone, another came through. Conveniently, it was from the male he needed.

Grinning, he answered. "Aw, honey, I was just thinking of you."

The responding snarl had him smiling wider. "What is going on down there?"

They were north of Terrence's compound, so down wasn't really accurate, but he wasn't ready to correct the Southeast Itan. Not when he needed something from the male. "Funny thing. I wanted to ask you the same."

"I'm getting calls, Reid. Never hear from Brookfield and now I'm suddenly getting calls all over the place."

"So am I. From you. Tell me who's being a little bitch and calling you instead of talking to me?" He needed to know so he could kick their ass. He had enough shit. He didn't need a tattletale siccing Terrence on him.

"I'm hearing shit I don't like."

"I'm seeing it," Reid countered. "And it ain't pretty." He sighed before going further. "I have no clue what happened here or what's been happening, but I've got a room full of women who look like they're ready to crawl out of their own skin if I look at 'em." He realized that wasn't unheard of when it came to him. "All right, they freak out if Asher looks at 'em."

"Damn," Terrence's whispered curse said it all. Asher was the closest thing to a puppy the bears had.

Bastard in a fight, but cute and cuddly when needed. That smile had more than one set of panties dropping. Evie's better not though. He should kill Asher in a preemptive strike.

"Yeah, so why don't you tell me—really tell me—why I'm here. What brought me here?" He didn't need to know what would keep him in Brookfield. It was about five-six, nice and curvy, with lips that tasted like strawberries and skin as pale as milk.

"Got a call on the hotline not quite a week ago. Five days. Mentioned that meat was spoiled and they needed heavy duty cleanup."

"Five days?" From what he understood, Evie was the one who called. Evie who they'd held in that basement, beating the shit out of her. Had she been there the whole time? "Why didn't you send me the second you got the call?"

"You were busy," Terrence drawled. "Getting your ass handed to you by your half-sister's mate."

Reid snorted. "I let that wolf win. He had to feel like the big man on his own land."

"But you let him really go at you which had you bitching about bruises and then somehow you got tied up in what you like to call 'family bullshit.'"

Wasn't that the truth? He'd grumbled and growled for days, but he secretly enjoyed the hell out of laughing kids and adults who weren't trying to figure out where best to stab someone. "You should have sent someone else, Terrence."

"I sent the best. I always send the best."

"You should have told me what I'd find."

"I gave you what I had, Reid. I'm sorry for whatever you found, for whatever anyone suffered because I didn't send you sooner." The bear sighed, the sound heavy and filled with regret. "If I'd known it was what you've described, I would have done more. My gut told me the clan needed the best. Wolf or not, you're it when it comes to wet work."

His gut clenched. Yeah, he was. More out of necessity than choice, but no one really knew that. They didn't understand what ran through his head when blood coated his hands. "I need any information you have about Brookfield. About the families here. About Patrick Archer's kids."

The rustle of papers reached him immediately followed by the beep and clicks from a computer. "Kids?" A handful more clicks. "He's single. Had a human mate who died under suspicious circumstances during childbirth. The child, a girl, passed as well. Patrick challenged his father not long after. He took over and surrounded himself with his brothers. Why? What do you see?"

Reid moved back to the office doorway and leaned against the frame. He spied the women, his men stationed around the room guarding them. Some kept their gazes trained on the windows and the land beyond while others zeroed in on the females. He wasn't worried—exactly—but he wouldn't relax until Ezekiel was gone. He liked killing just as much as the next shifter, sometimes a little too much. No one knew he had a purpose, a reason behind each and every slice and drop of blood he spilled.

To them, he was a monster.

In truth, they had no idea.

"I'm seeing Evelyn Archer, near thirty. Right next to her is Simone

Archer, just shy of twelve based on some of the documents I dug up in the office." He scanned the room, gaze falling on each guard one by one and making sure they were diligent. "I'm also seeing five women who are damn happy those three are gone." He lowered his voice and turned his head away from the group, fighting to be as quiet as possible. "More than one is pregnant, Terrence, and I have my own guesses about the fathers."

"Shit."

Yeah, shit.

"What did the caller say? What else am I looking at here?"

"Why don't you ask one of—"

"I'm not asking any of them anything yet. I'm taking control. I cleaned house and I'm making this place safe. I'll talk to them after I get things stable and Ezekiel dead."

"What about Clary? I could send her up there."

Nervous tension consumed his body as he thought about his therapist. He listened to her orders, not much choice since her opinion mattered to Terrence. But even beyond that, she was one scary bitch.

And shit, if she showed, she'd probably take something else away for killing the Archers. Like sex. If she grounded him from sex after he'd found Evie...

"No, I have it. Maybe later." After he had a few others on his side who could speak up for him. "We don't need to drag her into the middle of God's asshole."

Yes, he sounded like a pussy. Yes, he had reason. 'Nuff said.

"You sure? The callers have said…" All business but sounding so casual, telling Reid that Terrence didn't believe him. With good reason, but he wouldn't cop to that.

Well, calm was probably what the bear went for. But Reid heard the slight tremor that couldn't be attributed to cell reception. The small hitch in his breath and a hint of his heartbeat picking up its pace. Just because no one else could catch those sounds didn't mean they couldn't be heard.

It meant that others didn't have the training. They hadn't been raised in a house where survival hinged on listening and learning the way a male moved when he was happy or the speed at which he could lunge when he was furious.

"Not at this time."

Not ever if the woman continued to take shit away from him.

"Fine, anything else?"

Reid's gaze traveled through the main area of the house. Terrence sent him six of his best, but that wasn't enough to hold the clan and hunt for Ezekiel at the same time. "Another six bears. Wolves in a pinch. The clan has about sixty bears. I'd like to be able to out fight them if I need to."

"Something else going on I need to know about?"

"Nothing major. I gotta do some hunting, and I want everyone," — particularly Evie— "protected while I'm gone."

"Uh-huh."

"There aren't any local bears I trust." Staring at the women, looking at their wounded gazes and trembling bodies, he knew outside help was the only choice. "I don't know if the abuse was limited to the inner-circle. I won't let my clan be eaten up from inside while I'm distracted. Until I get shit cleaned up, I need your males. If you have to, grab some from my old pack. There are still a few crazy fuckers who wouldn't mind getting bloody."

"Compared to you, they're sane."

Reid grunted. "True enough."

"All right, anything else you need?"

Evie lifted her head, attention flitting around the room until her gaze landed on him. "Nope, I got everything else right here."

Chapter Seven

Evelyn didn't have to see Reid to know where he stood or when he moved through the house without saying a word. She sensed his retreat to Patrick's office and then heard the heavy thud of his boots as he reappeared and drew closer to the small cluster of women. And when the females went quiet, not even a whisper escaping their lips, she knew he was close.

A quick glance over her shoulder revealed she was right. He stood at her back, over six feet of heavy muscle and foreboding fewer than eight feet from them. He was frightening yet calming to Evelyn, her bear wary but interested in the massive male. She'd seen so much in the last weeks, witnessed so much violence, the mere thoughts had bile rising in her throat.

Yet knowing—witnessing—Reid's destruction didn't sicken her and she didn't know why.

Or rather, she did, she just didn't want to accept the truth. Was it a truth, though? His kiss rocked her to her core and her bear craved him like a fresh steak. That could be appreciation, a thankfulness that came from being saved. Was it more? Was it less?

Did she care? Did she care that she clung to him out of obligation and appreciation? That she wasn't sure she could even breathe with him out of sight. She'd been fine—fine—when he'd gone hunting, but his touch, that kiss, changed something. It twisted and turned and now—

"Evelyn." There was no question there. No rise in his voice that came with asking for someone's attention. It was flat. As if he expected her attention as his due.

And… her bear said he had every right. That they wanted him to demand control, take it. She slowly turned, unwilling to frighten the females in her haste to face him. Yet another quirk she'd never experienced. The hurry, the rush of desire to meet his gaze. "Yes?"

Reid jerked his head toward the back of the house and then turned to leave. No question. A demand.

Katherine clung to her hand, claw-tipped fingers digging into her skin and she gently extracted herself. She didn't wince with the sting as those nails sliced into her flesh. Katherine had more to worry about—the child growing inside her—than a few scratches on the dead Itan's daughter.

"Wait," the woman whimpered.

"I'll be right back," Evelyn gave her a small smile, trying to comfort her with the expression.

"No, you don't understand. I heard people talking. You don't know who he is," Katherine whispered the words as if she expected to be harmed for saying them aloud. "Wait."

Evelyn stopped trying to get away and paused, laying her palm atop Katherine's stiff hand. She met the female's gaze, imbuing the look with comfort and strength. "He's the one who saved Simone from our father. He's the one who saved the clan from my uncles. He's the one who will hunt Ezekiel and free us all. That's all I need to know."

"He's crazy," Katherine hissed.

"We're all a little crazy. Some hide it well; others don't bother." With that, she eased from the woman's hold and flicked her attention to Simone. They were a team now, two sisters against the crazy world they found themselves in. Things were different, unknown and unsteady, and they only had each other. Unless… She looked to the back of the den. Unless they had Reid as well.

Whispers followed her, but she ignored them in favor of walking in Reid's wake. She exchanged nods with a couple of the bears, their names forgotten, but she was sure she'd hear them once more. For now, she needed to focus on one particular wolf.

It was easy to find him, to scent his path to the back door and beyond into the yard. She spotted him leaning against the massive oak that threw shade across half the house, one foot flat on the ground and the other planted on the trunk.

He looked at ease in the world around him, but something teased her bear, niggled her mind and told her he was anything but relaxed. He was on edge, conscious of his surroundings and gaze flicking through the area as she approached. His wolf thrummed just beneath the surface and Evelyn's werebear reacted to his unease. It reared onto its back legs, lumbering forward and anxious to face a new threat.

"Reid?" What did he see? What did he feel?

Reid met her gaze and like a candle's flame, his emotions were locked down. The unease vanished between one breath and the next as if it'd never existed. His feelings were gone, leaving a blank mask in their place.

He extended his arm, hand open and fingers beckoning her. "C'mere."

Another order, not a question.

For some reason, Evelyn couldn't deny him and she padded forward, placing her hand in his and allowing herself to be drawn to him. He tugged until she was at his side, snuggled beneath his arm in a firm embrace. When he lowered his head, nose in her hair, and drew in a deep breath, that hold tightened further until she could hardly breathe. A rumbling growl soon followed, the sound skating over her nerves and the hair on her arms raised to goose bumps. They were a signal, a sign that his anger wasn't frustration but something more. Something harder and deeper and… frightening.

She'd told Katherine they were all crazy and that was the truth. What she didn't reveal was that she was sure Reid's insanity ran much deeper than what he revealed to the world.

It was deep, dark, deadly, and dirty. It reveled in blood and seemed to crave death. She'd seen a hint of it in the basement and heard the whispers of her father's passing.

There was more to Reid Bennett than a burning need to right the horrible wrongs.

"Who?" he rasped. She tilted her head back to meet his eyes. They were full amber though she was slowly becoming used to seeing his wolf so close to the surface. She'd only seen his natural brown once, when he spoke to Simone. As if he knew the amber frightened her little sister. "Who did it?"

"Did what?" And then his thumb skated over one of the small wounds, rough pad of his finger jarring the scrape. "Oh, that."

"That," he snapped. "Who was it? Who do I have—"

To kill. She knew the end of his sentence even if he cut it off.

"I'm fine."

"Bleeding is not fine. You bleeding is never fine." His touch roughened with each beat of his heart and every deep inhale. The more of her blood he scented, the more of his wolf stepped forward.

"Reid?" she whispered his name, hoping to break him out of his fixation on her wrist. She slipped from beneath his arm and placed her free hand on his cheek, urging him to meet her gaze. "Reid."

It was an order. He liked to give them often enough, she could issue one of her own. A movement to their right snared her attention for a moment and she met Asher's worried gaze. She shook her head in a short, gentle move, hoping to warn him off without Reid catching her, but she was unsuccessful.

With a snarl he released her, nudging her back in a fluid move as he spun and placed himself between her and Asher. "Get away from her." One flex had his wolf showing himself; claws out, fur coating his exposed skin and the snap of bone told her other parts of him adopted the animal as well. "Now."

Asher lifted his hands, palms out in a show of surrender. "I'm just checking on her, man. Katherine said you were looking pissed and—"

"I don't need you out here acting like a talking leash trying to keep me in line," he snarled, the sound booming through the air.

The bear didn't even wince or counter Reid's statement.

"You know what I'm here for, man."

A rumbling growl was Reid's only reply. The sound rolling in a gentle promise of pain and blood. But she wasn't afraid. Not like she'd been with her uncles. Theirs were deeper, darker, twisted, and perverted and they made her quake in her fur. Reid was worse than them. She knew it, felt it, but… it didn't scare her.

No, she hurt for him, for the distrust that followed him. She understood the looks now, the flickering hints of worry on the bears' faces that disappeared as quickly as they arrived.

They worked for Reid, listened to him, but didn't trust him.

"Reid," she whispered and stepped forward, pressing her front to his back. "Reid." She laid her hands on his shirt-covered back, fingers splayed on his shoulders. "Reid." She slid her palms to his arms, sliding them over his fur-covered muscles. "Reid." She let them wander down his biceps and to his forearms. "Reid." She encircled his wrists with her fingers. "Reid." She continued her journey and placed her fingers atop his, matching her small hand to his. "Reid." One last move, one last press of his hand as she forced his hands into fists and laid her cheek on the center of his back. "Reid."

The massive wolf shuddered, his chest expanding with a deep breath and then contracting in a slow exhale. With the action came a retreat of his fur, his muscles slowly decreasing and the carved lines gradually softening as the wolf's large form softened to his human shape. He carefully pulled his fists free of hers and just as gently encouraged her to wrap her arms around his waist. His fingers were petal soft when he stroked her skin and then his husky voice drifted through the air. The rumble vibrated through her as he spoke and she absorbed every word.

"Never, ever try to come between us. Never, ever approach me when I am holding her. Never, ever test me in such a way again because I cannot guarantee she could keep me from killing you."

Asher's swallow was audible, not even the birds daring to counter

Reid. "I understand."

The bear's steps were quiet as he retreated, leaving them alone, and neither moved while the silence descended. Reid carefully turned, shifting until her chest was flush with his. Then he hugged her, thick arms encircling her in a gentle hug—a move that contrasted with the wolf's air of danger and violence and she didn't think many saw this side of him.

"Don't do that again," he rumbled and she let his voice sink into her.

"What?" she whispered.

"Try to stop me."

"Why?" She would always save him, even from himself.

"Because I can't guarantee I won't kill you."

Chapter Eight

Shit, he wished he had a smoke. Just one. Hell, he wouldn't even have to light it up. Simply hold it and think and try to figure out his fuck up.

I can't guarantee I won't kill you.

It was the truth, but he probably should have said it a little nicer. Or... not said it at all. Clary would have urged him to work through his emotions and shit and do some anger cleansing exercises. Then she would have taken away... something. Or prescribed yoga. He hated yoga.

Gutting Asher was exercise. He'd enjoy it. Unlike yoga.

Had he mentioned he hated yoga?

Instead of gutting Asher, he sat on the front porch not smoking or drinking coffee because Clary was a bitch, while waiting for Terrence's guys to make their appearance. He didn't expect them for a while—around lunchtime and the sun was only rising above the mountains—but sat outside anyway. He wouldn't admit he was hiding from Evie. Had been since yesterday. He didn't want to see her disgust or fear after their confrontation with Asher.

He wished he could apologize for what he said, claim the words were nothing more than anger fueling his actions and he wouldn't really hurt her. He wished he could make that promise, but history told him there was no way he could make that vow. Not when he was pretty sure he'd break it if shoved too hard. He shied from those memories, from the time he was pushed and he pushed back.

He settled on the top step, watching the day break while keeping his eyes on the tree line. Around five, he'd sent three males into the forest to hunt for Ezekiel—hoping the male came back to search for their weaknesses—and none had called in with good news. Ezekiel had vanished and not a peep was heard. Didn't bother Reid, though. Zeke would turn up and that was when Reid would take him down. Quick and easy. Hopefully bloody.

Then… then he didn't know what he'd do. He knew what he wanted, but wanting and getting were two different things. In Reid's world they never coincided. Didn't mean he wouldn't hope he'd get his way this time around. Mainly because he wasn't sure he could walk away if Terrence decided Reid was needed elsewhere and gave the clan to another.

Terrence giveth and taketh away. A bit sacrilegious, but Terrence was god to this corner of the U.S.

The first clue a newcomer came near was the soft patter of feet on wood inside the house. Then the low squeak of the front door and the groan of the screen's hinges. That patter picked up on the porch and didn't stop until she stood beside him. She.

Reid recognized each sound, cataloged it, but it was her scent that truly had him acknowledging her presence. He tilted his head back, exposing his throat to her in a move that surprised him. Anyone else and he'd roll to his feet to meet them eye to eye. With her? He made himself vulnerable, he told her without words that his life was in her hands and she could end it if she desired.

"Hi." Smooth, Reid, smooth.

"Hi," her voice was soft and questioning. Uneasy, unsure and… unacceptable.

The wolf growled and grumbled at her tone, forcing him to take action. Part of him knew he should drive her away, hurt her, and make her run from him. The other part, the part ruled by the animal and its base desires, told him to draw her close and destroy any that threatened their… mating.

Mate. The word flooded his blood. Mate. The word filled his heart. Mate. The word resonated in his soul and he was forced to accept it.

Mine wasn't an abstract concept, it was a bone deep truth and he couldn't avoid the realization any longer.

She belonged to him and he'd defend that ownership until death.

And he knew she felt the same. At least somewhat. Some part of her had to see she belonged to him as well.

Yet... she was a half-shifter. Something he knew from her scent and his talk with Terrence. If her feelings didn't match his, he'd make sure they did eventually through whatever means necessary short of hurting her.

He couldn't harm his mate to save his life.

That thought immediately calmed his unease from earlier.

I can't guarantee I won't kill you. Yes, he could give her that guarantee.

Reid reached for her, snaring her hand and drawing her down beside him. No, that wasn't close enough. Not nearly. He continued his pull until she rested on one thigh, her head immediately nestling onto his shoulder and her face against his neck.

His wolf rumbled with his happiness, the animal overjoyed at her closeness. It didn't want to let her out of its sight. Not now. Not ever.

"What are you doing out here on your own?" She didn't raise her voice, her question soft like a gentle wind.

"Better question is why you're risking your life by getting close to me?"

She smiled against his neck. "Because I don't really think you'll hurt me."

"That's not what everyone else says."

Evie went quiet and he wasn't sure she'd speak again. Didn't really matter though. He had her close and that's all he cared about. "Everyone else hasn't seen what I've seen."

Wasn't that the truth? "They're still going to give you shit. They're still going to cling to your arm when you leave them and come to me."

That was the only explanation he could come to when he'd spied the nicks in her arm. Someone objected—firmly—to her following him.

"They can say—and do—whatever they want." She shrugged. "It won't change anything." When she pulled away from him, their gazes clashed. "Are you going to harm anyone in the clan?"

"Not unless they deserve it. I won't let men like your uncles live and I won't apologize for their deaths."

"Then we don't have a problem." She said it like it was that simple.

Sometimes the easiest things are the hardest.

"You can't believe that."

"I can," she shrugged. "I," she shook her head. "You know what? I grew up happy. I had my grandmother's clan—"

"Your father's mother?"

She shook her head. "No, my mom's. She was mostly human, enough that most considered her human, but my family has enough that my grandmother was welcome at the local clan's gatherings. When I came, I spent a lot of time with those bears." She paused for a moment, gathering her thoughts. "I was happy if picked on." The urge to destroy every person who made Evie cry reared up in him and a soft whisper of his name had him settling. "I was still happy. It was normal kid stuff."

He grunted and she continued.

"I had a good childhood. I had support when I went to medical school and even more when my grandmother became ill and I had to come home early. When she passed..." Moisture gathered in her eyes and a single tear slipped down her cheek. He didn't really have a handle on the whole comforting thing, but he tried anyway.

He brushed away the salty liquid and rubbed her hand in small circles. "Her will forced me to come here. She thought it was time to return to my birth clan. Grandma took me when I was younger, worried about whoever killed my mother, and then I stayed. Now, with the will, the Itan couldn't deny her last request and my fath— Patrick wanted me to come. He was nice on the phone, smooth when he talked to my Itan." Another tear, another gentle swipe.

"I know what happiness is. I know what goodness is. And now I know what pure evil looks like. I saw it every day for weeks. I saw it every time I opened my eyes and heard it with every scream." She shook her head, dislodging a few soft curls until they framed her heart-shaped face. "I see anger and pain in your eyes, but I don't see evil, Reid." She leaned toward him, forehead on his as she whispered. "I see what you try to show others, but I don't believe it. Not for a second."

"You should." He didn't want her looking close, didn't want her digging into places she didn't belong. Evie… saw too much.

"No, I shouldn't."

This close, her scent enveloped him, consuming him and sinking into every inch of his body. His wolf howled its appreciation, urging him to take her, to capture her and drag her to their den. The house at their back belonged to them now. They were strong enough to evict everyone within its walls and then they'd have Evie to themselves.

It was tempting, a thought and desire that grew with each passing second. He wanted her alone, wrapped around him and only focused on him.

"Evie," he spoke her name with a growl, his beast filling him and stretching the edge of his control.

"Evelyn," her correction was a soft tease.

"You should go." But he didn't push her away. Physically couldn't move her from him. His muscles refused to react to his choice and the wolf retained control of his body.

"What happened to you?"

"Terrence called me. I came. I killed, and now I'm the Itan."

"I'm not talking recently. I'm talking about the past. That's not what I mean and you know it."

He did. Funny thing though. No one knew the truth. Not his family, not Clary, and he sure as hell didn't tell Terrence.

But fuck him sideways, he wanted to tell Evie. Everything. Every word and emotion. Every strike of pain and every tear he'd shed. The first day... God, that day he'd let them go, let them wash away the blood on his hands.

And then never again.

"Evie..." It was a warning and plea in one. If she kept pushing and prodding, he'd cut open the old wound and let it bleed for her. He'd give it all, lay his past in her hands, and let her judge him. It'd hurt, it'd probably come close to killing him, but he'd do it. For her. For a woman he hardly knew and couldn't breathe without. "I..."

The rumble reached him first, the sound nearly imperceptible, but present nonetheless. He tilted his head to the side and closed his eyes, listening and he was thankful his mate—for she could be nothing else—remained silent. A vehicle. No, two. Large. SUVs? Their kind—shifters—tended to only drive bigger trucks. They hated being confined.

If it wasn't for the fact he knew Terrence was big on early mornings and demanded his bears be the same, he'd be worried about who crested the hill. But he knew who drew nearer.

Reid gave Evie's leg a gentle squeeze and encouraged her to stand as he did the same.

Asher burst through the front door, wide grin on his face and cell phone in his hand. "Just talked to Terrence. Looks like he sent these guys early, but said the love of your life is throwing a bitch fit about you not answering her calls and being denied permission to come to Brookfield."

Two things happened then. Evie stiffened, her surprise and hurt coating him in a disgusting wave that had his stomach cramping and wolf howling. He also decided Asher was better off dead.

Evie stepped away from him, putting space between them, and he hated it. He reached for her, growling low when she eased just out of reach. "Evie—"

"I bet Terrence won't be able to keep her away for long and she'll be here by nightfall."

Dead. The male was dead.

Chapter Nine

Other than getting in and out of the SUV, Reid hadn't released Evelyn since they'd left the den. Just as the two SUVs rolled to a stop, he grabbed her hand and hauled her toward the first large vehicle. Then he'd basically ripped a male out of the passenger seat before doing the same to the driver. The other bear managed to scramble from the truck before Reid peeled down the driveway.

Now he tugged her down Main Street toward the local diner. He'd heard it was a favorite among the bears, the owners serving mostly meat with occasionally a side of hash browns at breakfast or French fries at lunch. Nothing green crossed the threshold of Come and Get It. Ever.

"Reid?" She tried to snare his attention, but he just grunted in response. "Reid?" She spoke louder and tugged against his hold, trying to get him to stop or slow or something other than pull her like he was three and she was his favorite red wagon.

"Reid," she yanked herself free of his strangling grip and he spun to face her, yellowed eyes out in full force. His expression was just short of a snarl, but she wasn't afraid of him. He was frustrated and angry but not at her. "Reid, what's going on?" She tried for gentle and she wasn't sure she was successful. Not when she realized she had her own fangs filling her mouth. Apparently her bear didn't like his glare and was letting Evelyn know.

Great.

He jerked back, eyes still narrow but some of his rough anger receded and he turned his attention to their surroundings. A glance around them had him changing direction and he pulled her toward the alley between the diner and hardware store.

Then she was in his arms, his massive hands pulling and tugging until she found her back flush with a brick wall and Reid surrounding her with his presence. He caged her, enveloping her in his body and scent, and her bear rumbled in approval. It liked this Reid, liked him tugging and pushing her as he desired; asserting his dominance without demanding her subjugation. He didn't taunt or tease or hurt her for no reason. He demanded and her bear was more than willing to give over to his desires.

"He..." Reid growled low and she immediately stroked him, hands reaching for his skin and mentally wincing when she found fur. "I don't love her. Don't like her. She's a necessity and I need you away from that and if she tries to get close and you pull away because of her..." He shook his head. "She won't make it to morning. I won't let anything hurt you. Not ever."

"Who? Who is she to you? To me?" She readily admitted Asher's words cut deeply, slicing her to her core.

...love of your life...

Reid pressed his cheek to her neck, burying his face in her hair as he drew in a deep breath and then released it slowly. Another inhale and gradual exhale, each one stirring the strands. "Not here. Not now."

"Where then? When?" She needed an explanation. Her bear craved the words. Not because she didn't trust in this driving force shoving them together, but to protect her own heart. She slowly accepted they belonged together, but if his heart was tied to another.

She wasn't sure how she'd survive.

Another wheezing inhale was followed by a soft sigh. He crowded her closer, one thigh slipping between hers and she easily moved with him, moving as he desired until she found her legs lifted and wrapped around his waist. She slipped her arms behind his neck and clung to him as he continued to breathe through whatever anger— and fear?—plagued him.

Something sent him running. Something about that woman, and Evelyn's bear resolved to kick the female out of Brookfield the moment she could. What they had was built on violence and death, but she hoped to continue creating something that didn't involve blood and gore or... heartache. She wasn't sure which was worse, the killing or the crying she saw on the horizon.

"Evie..." he whispered her name and she didn't bother correcting him. She wouldn't admit that she liked the nickname from his lips. Ever. "I need a day, an hour, just time without them. Without the fight, without the bears."

"I hate to state the obvious," she drawled. "But I'm a bear."

He shook his head. "No, you're so much more. You don't expect me to lead your ass around like a young one."

That made her feel good and hurt at the same time. "Is that what you think of my clan?"

Hers. Hers since she took a punch for them. A kick for them. A claw for them. Scars littered her body and they were for each one of the souls in the Brookfield clan.

"Right now? They're so beat down, Evie. They are like pups. Lost. Scared. And I understand, but I need five minutes with you. With your scent and touch. Need it like air before we talk about my bullshit."

"Reid?" The deep baritone was familiar, but she couldn't place the male's name. All she knew was he invaded their space and destroyed the moment between her and her mate.

Unfortunately for the newcomer, Reid took the interruption worse than Evelyn. She only groaned. Reid roared. Louder than a bear, hell, scarier than any shifter she'd heard. The sound reminded her of a lion yet so much more.

The scuffle of a boot on asphalt drew her attention to the street and the pale bear who'd dropped to his knees, neck bared. The man's breathing came in heavy pants and the wind brought the stench of fear to them.

Evelyn sifted her fingers through his hair, fisting the strands and giving them a soft tug to grab his attention. "You realize I'm spending more time calming you than I do just talking to you."

Reid grunted and she realized it was his go-to response when he didn't have anything to say.

She tugged again and he drew his gaze from the kneeling bear to her. "What's his name?"

He glared at her, a quick look of possessiveness crossing his features as he curled his lip. "Carter."

"I don't recognize him. Who is he to the clan?"

"From Grayslake. One of the bears I hauled outta the SUV. Wants to be a guard in Brookfield."

"And your first thought when he interrupted?"

Reid's attention drifted back to the kneeling bear, and he bared his fangs fully. "Mine."

Evelyn sighed and pushed back her arousal. His near-violent possessiveness was sexy. And dangerous. She saw some of what others whispered about, but she recognized it for what it was. Reid wasn't insane. Her uncles—her father—were crazed. They did things for the fun of the pain and nothing more.

Reid just had a very black and white look at life. His emotions were fierce, fast, and unforgiving. And when he made a choice, he reveled in it. It was the reveling that squicked people out.

"And he won't challenge that. Do you think anyone would try to take something you claimed?"

Reid froze for a moment and took a slow breath. Fur receded as he released the air in his lungs and his muscles lost some of their tenseness. "No. If they tried, they'd die."

"I'm pretty sure Carter didn't wake up this morning looking to be dead by breakfast." She focused on the bear. His neck was still exposed, but some of his fear lessened. "Am I right?"

"Yes, Ita—" Reid's growl cut the bear off.

"You could let him finish." She poked Reid.

"I could also kill him for looking at you."

And there went the male's fear again.

"We need to talk about this. I won't be silenced because your wolf gets pissy."

Once again she was the focus of his glare. "People don't argue with me."

Evelyn raised a single brow. "Really? Good thing I'm not people. I'm your mate."

He grunted. "At least you know and admit it."

"I admit you're being a jerk, too." She tilted her head toward the end of the alley. "He's still kneeling and I know from experience it's not a comfortable position."

Another grunt.

"Let him up."

"He's weaker."

"Doesn't mean you have to be an asshole about it."

He pressed his lips together. "Did you just call me an asshole?"

"No, I said you're being an asshole. There's a difference." Not much of one, but there was. Of course, she'd tried explaining that to her father and the first time she said it to anyone in the clan was the last time. That was when she'd learned the pain of kneeling on rocks and asphalt. For hours. Not the worst punishment, it didn't involve blood, but one she remembered clearly.

"You gonna be like this the rest of our lives?"

"You mean call you on your bullshit and keep you from flipping out for no reason?"

The look she received was fierce and filled with an urgency and determination she hadn't seen from him. "There is always a reason. No one may understand them when the time comes for action, but there's a reason."

And she believed him.

"Okay," she easily agreed. "I'll always support you, Reid. You just may need to stop and explain things now and again." She tilted her head toward the still kneeling Carter. "Your bear came to check on you. To make sure we were okay after we tore out of the driveway. Because that's his job. He's meant to take care of the clan and that includes you. So he's got your back and when he thinks you need help, he's gonna step up."

He didn't say a word, so she kept going. "And if that's not what you want, you need to explain it. Snarling won't solve the problem. It instills fear. When you need him next, he won't know if he should come forward or hang back and that could end up with you dead." Reid snorted so she upped the stakes. "Or me."

That had him reacting with a rumbling growl, the sound deep and threatening as if danger and death stood before them. "Never."

"Then tell him why he should have stayed back. You say you have to lead the clan as if they were children. Well, act like a damned parent, then."

"I don't like your tone."

She rolled her eyes. "And I don't like that you're being a dick, so we're even."

Carter, god love the male, snorted.

So not a good idea, Carter.

"Reid?"

"What?" he snapped, glare still on the kneeling bear.

"Tell Carter to get the hell out of here because I'm hungry. You can explain things to the guards later."

He huffed and finally spoke. "Fine," he grumbled. "Carter, you can go. If I'm with Evie and you scent pain, fear, or violence, you interrupt. Otherwise, I will gut you where you stand and send a letter of apology along with your body when I return it to your family. We clear?"

Carter's swallow was audible. "Yes, Itan."

Reid grunted and Evelyn felt the need to translate. "Thank you, Carter. We'll see you later." The male immediately rolled to his feet and disappeared from sight, leaving them alone once more. And… that was about the time her stomach growled. "Feed me, Reid. Then explain why the love of your life is itching to come to the den and could show up at any second."

He curled his lip, disgust replacing the anger in his scent. "Love her? I hate her. Would have killed her a long time ago if I didn't need her."

"Who is she?" Evelyn raised her eyebrows, hoping he'd answer.

Another grunt. Then a sigh. "My therapist."

Chapter Ten

Evelyn didn't look at him like he was crazy. That was always a plus.

She also kept him from gutting Carter for interrupting, which meant Clary wouldn't come down hard on him for killing someone. Again. He already had three strikes against him, and then when he found Ezekiel…

Unfortunately, telling Evie about Clary meant he had to explain other shit. The thought of that, of revealing himself to her, made his skin itch and the wolf pressed forward. It wanted to talk even less than him.

Evie wiggled, reminding him he had his mate wrapped around him all warm and sexy and he really wanted to get to know her… intimately.

And he wasn't talking about talking.

Her stomach grumbled, reminding him she was hungry. He might be an asshole but he wasn't negligent. Wolf wanted to feed her more than he wanted to hide.

"C'mon," he grumbled. "Lemme get some food in you."

Hating every second of it, Reid lowered her to the ground, carefully easing her legs from his waist and holding her tightly until she took her own weight. She was still pressed intimately against him, those curves snug to his body, and he absorbed her heat, basking in their closeness. And her scent. So sweet and musky, it consumed him, aroused him, and gave him a satisfaction he'd never known.

He had plenty of women in his past but Evie was everything they weren't—his.

Forcing himself into motion, he stepped away and put some space between their bodies. Otherwise he'd pin her to the wall once more and take everything she offered. Hell, if she was game, he'd claim her then and there. Take her in front of every male in town so they'd know she belonged to him.

He didn't do that sharing shit.

Grabbing her hand, he led them back to the street and resumed his path, pulling her toward the only diner in town. All reports said the food was decent, if simple, but a shifter just needed meat to be happy, so he figured Come and Get It was good enough for now. Later he'd wine and dine her, give her everything she deserved.

Like, after he destroyed the last threat and slit Ezekiel's throat. He'd tear the male into tiny pieces first. Clawing his flesh from bone seemed like a good idea. Maybe—

A light tug on his hand had him abandoning his ideas and focusing on Evie once more. He met her gaze and raised a single eyebrow. "Yeah?"

She rolled her eyes. "We can't eat unless we go inside. Funny how that works."

Evie wasn't afraid of him. At all.

And he loved that shit.

Reid just snorted and snagged the door, pulling it open so she could go ahead of him.

"Brat," he murmured in her ear as she passed and got a smile in response.

"And?"

He shrugged. "And nothing."

"Hmm..." She strode into the diner and waved at the woman behind the counter.

The woman first smiled widely at Evie in welcome until she met his gaze and then that grin vanished as if it'd never existed. That earned him a flick on the arm from Evie. "What?" he grumped. "Not my fault your bears wanna piss themselves when they meet me."

"Yeah, it is." Then she softly patted his chest. "But don't worry. I'll fix it."

"What if I don't want shit fixed?"

Midnight eyes met his gaze and her voice dropped. "You do. I know you do. Even if you won't say it out loud."

He wasn't saying shit out loud. Ever. Not around these people.

Instead of answering, he nudged her toward an empty booth at the back of the diner. "C'mon. Need to eat."

The diner quieted as they made their way through the building to the table he'd chosen, conversations going silent and not picking up until they passed. Evie seemed to think that kind of shit would end eventually.

He didn't want to tell her she was wrong, it'd never happen. When she smiled at him, those plump lips parting with joy and happiness filling her eyes, he decided he wouldn't tell her anything for a long while.

Eventually they found their way to the booth and Reid slipped in, his back to the wall and eyes able to see the whole diner. If someone came at him, he sure as hell wasn't gonna make it easy.

Evie didn't seem to notice—or pretended not to notice—that the diner was a hell of a lot quieter now than when they'd arrived. Nope, she snatched up her menu as if everything was normal and skimmed the list of available food.

Meanwhile, Reid kept his attention trained on the room at large, gaze drifting over the open area as he searched for any threat. His bears—a couple from Grayslake that filed in after them and a few Brookfield natives—filled over half the place while the rest were humans. Humans who sensed enough to be wary.

Smart.

"What do you want?" Evie's soft question brought him back to her.

"What?"

"Food? What do you want? This is the shifter menu, but I can ask for the other if you'd like."

"Beef." Deer in a pinch, but Reid was a sucker for a cow. Screw chicken. They were a pain in the ass to hunt and bland when compared to a nice steak.

"Burger? Fajitas? Tacos?" She raised her eyebrows and he finally glanced at the menu. Damn, the Brookfield bears cooked their beef in more ways than he could count. Hell, they had a nice deer menu, too.

And duck. Well, at least duck wasn't chicken and it had some nice fat on it.

Then he got to... "The fuck?" He curled his lip and met Evie's stare. "Fruit?"

"You're mating a bear, Reid." She rolled her eyes. "We do enjoy more than one food group."

A high-pitched squeak followed by an equally high-pitched "mate?" had both of them looking at the newcomer. A woman, all curves and curls that would have drawn him before he met Evie, stood nearby. Her stained apron and nametag had him pegging her as their waitress.

Evie turned in her seat and his mate's smile lit up the whole place. "Lottie, how are you?"

"Evelyn, is he your... You..." Reid scented the air, drawing in the surrounding scents and realized the woman was human. Mostly. She had a little something extra in there that he couldn't quite place. The female shook her head and then sadness and pity filled her gaze. "Your poor face."

That had the smile on his mate's lips vanishing in an instant, one fluttering hand raising to draw her hair forward.

Screw that.

Reid growled low, the rumble starting deep in his soul and slinking forward until it vibrated the air in the entire diner. The shifters dropped their gazes, necks bared, while the humans huddled close to one another.

The waitress held her ground—barely—and squeezed her eyes shut.

He kept the sound going, rolling on and on until… Evie half-stood, reached across the table and flicked his ear. "Dammit, woman."

"Quit. It's fine. I…" She swallowed hard, face paling as her fingers traced the scarring. "I forgot. That's all. I'm just not used to them yet, but I'll get over it."

"You shouldn't have to," he grumbled. "None of them should say a motherfucking word about those scars." He glared at the room, his fury eating at him. "That shit happened because not a single one of them would speak up. No one made the call. How long did it take, Evie? To make a call and leave a message?"

"Reid…" she whispered and he shook his head, fighting the bile that rose in his throat.

Wolf liked blood as much as the next shifter, but the memories of Evie's covering the tile made him sick. "No. You made a call and suffered for it. They tortured you, Evie, and I'm not gonna sit here while the assholes start making you feel like you're not gorgeous because of 'em."

"She's not—"

"I'm not judging her and she still is beautiful. I can feel bad that she was in pain, though," the waitress snapped and he had to admire the woman's grit. "And I can apologize that she felt it, but that's it. I resent the implication."

If the woman had fangs he imagined she would have snapped them at him.

"Lottie!" Someone hissed and then a massive male, more pudge than muscle, tugged her away. He was older, with graying hair and quite a few wrinkles. Father or grandfather. The scent was similar and yet…

It clicked.

Reid grinned and turned his attention to Evie. "That mouse has one hell of a roar."

The mouse's squeak came a split second before Lottie was back again. "And if you think—"

He shook his head, not sure what was wrong with him, but his normal fury that came from disrespect was nowhere to be seen.

Because she may be defending herself, but she's standing up for Evie and the clan too. Gotta respect that. Especially from a mouse.

"I think I'm hungry and my mate is eyeing that fruit platter."

The mouse glared at him, beady eyes narrowed, but spun on her heel and disappeared behind a set of swinging doors, the older male flashing Reid the same look before chasing after her.

With them gone, he refocused on Evie, wondering what he'd have to say if she still had that sad, wounded look in her eyes. Except he found her grinning widely, the worst of her scars tugging at her lips, but not marring her beauty.

"What?" he barked.

"Nothing." The grin remained.

"What are you smiling at then?" The shit made him uncomfortable.

"You. You got pissy and didn't threaten to eat her for lunch."

He shrugged and refused to talk about why. "She's not enough for a snack let alone lunch."

Another squeak, this one from the other side of the room but it didn't sound so mouse-like. More like frightened human.

Evie laughed, the sound tinkling and filled with happiness. "You don't mean that."

He glared. He didn't and he hated that she knew that. "You think you know me."

She shook her head, that dreamy smile he really loved in place. "I don't need to know you, not all of you, to know you weren't a threat to her."

"You sure about that?" Because he sure as hell wasn't.

"Yeah," there was so much faith and shit in her expression. Like she believed what she was saying and... dammit, he wanted to be that man for her. "Yeah, I really am sure."

Well, shit.

Chapter Eleven

That was how the rest of the afternoon went. Reid growling and Evelyn poking and prodding him, showing the clan that he wasn't all bad, just snarly.

And it was exhausting. She liked the guy—inched toward more than liking him—but her mate saw everyone as a threat. Everyone. Even Sam in the hardware store who had to be near eighty and half-blind.

Sam threatened to put Reid over his knee. Reid threatened to rip out his heart…

Good times.

They walked up Main Street, popping into the salon and antique store, pausing at the grocers and then at the pharmacy next door followed by… the family doctor's office. Oh, they had other physicians around their small town. Even a handful of specialists (no pregnant woman wanted to drive to the next town to have her vagina checked). But when locals said, "I'm going to the doctor," that doctor was Doc Hill. Old, decrepit, and wily.

And also the only one who agreed to consider helping her with her residency. She'd graduated medical school, but was sent to Brookfield before all was said and done.

Evelyn put her hand on the door, swinging it wide before Reid had a chance to tug it open for her. She knew frustration was slowly becoming his middle name and she wanted in and out before he squished the elderly human.

She strode in, Reid on her heels. "Are you sick?"

"No." She gave him a small smile over her shoulder. "You know I'm fine. Just sore."

He grunted. She'd slowly come to learn those sounds. That one was fuck, yeah, I know. Yes, he always cursed in her interpretations. They had to be true to him, after all.

"Then why are we here?"

"I just need a sec." Hopefully alone because if Doc Hill denied her request...

She padded to the receptionist desk to speak with Trisha, ignoring Reid's grumbles. What she couldn't ignore was his heat and the way his scent wrapped around her when he stepped close. "Is Dr. Hill available? I'd like to speak to him about—"

"You," the doctor barked. "I told you no."

Trisha sighed. "No, Dr. Hill. You told her to come back another time because Timmy Mitchum was screaming his head off and—"

The doctor grunted. "That was three weeks ago." He narrowed his eyes and lifted his glasses, staring at her through the thick lenses. "Seems the weeks haven't been good to ya."

Anytime anyone mentioned her injuries, Reid growled and bared his teeth, which made Evelyn sigh. "I—"

"You do that to her?" Doc Hill waved his finger at her but stared at her mate.

"You dare—" Reid stepped forward and she bolted around him and planted her feet, doing her best to keep the two men separated.

"No, he didn't and the guys who did left town."

Left town. Right.

A grunt from the doc. "He take care of them, then? Heard your daddy and uncles ran off. Them the ones who did that?"

"Yes, Reid ran Dad, Daniel, and Sean off." Or into the ground. Whatever.

"That's what they're calling it these days then." He shrugged. "In my day, your granddaddy would get the town together for the bonfire. He only took out the mean pieces of work, so we were pretty damned happy about it and then there was the barbeque after. Not the men. They brought in a pig for that, but—"

"You knew my grandfather? He wasn't…An evil piece of shit?

"Course. I'm old. Don't mean I want you reminding me, but I am. He'd like you a little bit. Wouldn't like that you haven't finished your learning, but I'll take care of it." The doc dropped his glasses back to his nose. "Owed him fifty when he died. I'll repay him this way."

"Seriously?" Evelyn raised her eyebrows.

The doc put his hands in his pockets and rocked back on his heels. "Yup, gonna call it even."

"Because you owe her dead grandfather fifty bucks, you're gonna let Evelyn work here?" Reid sounded as confused as she was, but Evelyn didn't want to get into it with the old man. He might just change his mind.

"Yup, may even pay her for it."

The pop and tinkle of shattering glass reached her before she realized what happened. Then another, and another. Somewhere amidst those sounds came a heavy weight slamming into her, sending her crashing to the ground with a low grunt. Pain shot through her, the body atop hers digging into some of her lingering wounds that still ached.

Those pops were now accompanied by thumps and a rain of plaster and drywall. She lifted her head and stared at the new holes in the wall, the circles scattered across the surface and her mind slowly put the pieces of the puzzle together.

Someone was shooting at them. With guns.

Someone was shooting at them with guns.

A deep, masculine groan came from above her and another from across the room followed by a whimper from behind the desk.

Then the scent of blood teased her nose, the aroma coppery yet tinged with a sting she couldn't identify. It pestered her mind, dancing in and out of her thoughts, taunting her with the knowledge she needed. The smell was foreign, not related to oil or gunpowder.

Her bear roared with its presence, shouting and snarling that it was wrong, it was bad, and the source of that sting needed to get out of him.

But she couldn't find the knowledge in her brain. God. It was shifter-related. She knew that. While she'd learned human biology, she was also mentored by her local clan Healer.

What did he say? What did he say?

More groaning, another whimper.

It didn't matter. She had patients and no one else was going to help her.

Evelyn carefully eased from beneath Reid's bulk, careful to jar him as little as possible. He'd protected her and if he was injured, it was most likely on his back. Just as she slipped free, the rapid pounding of booted feet announced a newcomer.

She swung her attention to the front door as Carter burst into the office. She spied another few males behind the bear, a couple she recognized as part of the Brookfield clan but the others were new and thankfully the Grayslake bears outnumbered the local clan. She wasn't sure about the Brookfield bears, but she felt like she could trust those sent by the Southeast Itan.

"Carter, go to the back, find whatever medical supplies you can. I need gauze, forceps, and scissors. He's probably got his morphine and other drugs locked up." She looked to the male at his left. A familiar face. "Asher, find the cabinet and tear it open. Bring syringes and whatever you find. Don't check labels just grab it all. I'll look through 'em when you get back." The two males continued to stare at her with wide eyes. "Go!" she roared and they bolted into action.

Evelyn focused on Reid and then Doc Hill before rising and heading around the desk to check on Trisha. She was crying, whimpering as she leaned against the wall. She had her hand pressed tightly to a shoulder wound. Painful, not deadly.

Evelyn stood and snapped her fingers at yet another bear, this one from Brookfield. Damn, they had more tailing them than she realized. "You, put pressure on her wound."

This one didn't hesitate to rush forward and do as she demanded. At least they were learning.

She moved on to Reid and Doc Hill, quickly doing a physical sweep of the men, determining who needed her more at a glance.

Only Doc Hill gave her directions. "Only got a flesh wound. Burns like hell, though. Feels like they dipped those bullets in hellfire."

The shatter of glass and slam of cabinets preceded Carter and Asher's appearance.

Then she really used her training. She'd never worked in an emergency setting, but when push came to shove, her body and mind gave her the answers she needed. She cut away fabric or ordered it done. Used gauze to clean areas, dug out bullets, and fought to ignore the sounds of her patients. She managed to unearth local anesthetic and needles, so eventually the receptionist was numbed, which left her with the doc and Reid.

Doc was a bad patient, but Reid was worse.

The male wouldn't stay still, grumbling and growling with each prod. Blood flowed freely from the wounds, continuing to coat her fingers and... the next time he glanced over his shoulder at her, snarl on his lips, she realized his eyes were glassy.

Pupils wide.

Slow to respond.

Sluggish speech.

Fear and panic warred within her, pumping into her veins and increasing her adrenaline levels until her body knew what she needed before her mind processed the necessity.

Help. Knowledge.

Doc Hill shouted about burning.

Reid's eyes turned glassy and unfocused.

Trisha's wounds still bled—sluggishly but continuously.

"Dr. Hill?"

"What?" He wheezed and a quick glance revealed his wound was in roughly the same shape, blood now soaking his white lab coat and flowing from the gash in his arm.

Without a beat, she rattled off her question, outlining the consistent facts between the three of them.

"Told you it's hellfire, girl."

"Oh, shit," Asher whispered. "Oh, shit. I know what this is." The stench of his panic overrode all other scents. Then he was yelling, demanding, sending men racing to the grocers for baking soda and...

"Asher?"

Wide eyes met her gaze, his face pale and he wiped off his hand before lifting it. She transferred her attention to his fingers and palm, noting the raw skin and blistering that slowly became visible. "Carvrix. It's... I remember it from Grayslake. The hyenas and the Healer's mate and they nearly died and—"

The door banged open and in raced two bears, both clutching boxes and boxes of baking soda.

"Pour a box on Reid, the doc, and the receptionist. Then dilute a box in water. Bring the pitcher back. Don't stop until we say. Keep 'em coming."

"Asher?" Her heart froze. Nearly died? She stared at the man beside her. His breathing came in soft, shallow breaths and his skin was coated in more and more blood. And the wounds seemed to grow in size, spreading and deepening as time passed and—

Rough hands shoved an opened box at her. "Do it or he'll die. The poison won't stop. It'll keep eating until it's neutralized."

His tone was harsh and similar to what she'd heard from more than one emergency room doctor as he barked orders and demanded obedience as if it was his due. She didn't miss the conviction in his words and she took a chance, leapt and prayed that Asher was right, that she could trust him to save... her mate.

She found him—he'd found her—and she couldn't lose him now.

So she tipped the box over his back, sprinkling it into the six bullet holes marring his flesh. The white powder quickly turned red as it soaked up the fluid. She wiped away the excess, wanting a clear view of the deep gashes.

Then the bears were back, sloshing pitchers of cloudy water. Carter held two, quickly passing one to her while handing off the second to Asher. The third male disappeared behind the desk with a soft murmur, almost a comforting coo followed by a softly whispered I'm sorry. No one else was supposed to get hurt.

Evelyn shook her head. She didn't have time to delve into the bear's behavior or continue listening to his words. Right then, she had a mate to worry about. Because as she waited for the baking soda to go to work and stop the spreading damage, his breaths became softer, hardly a rise and fall of his chest as time ticked past. She poured the liquid over his back, washing away the sticky evidence of her first attempt to heal him. Now it was pitcher after pitcher, soaking the carpet with bloodstained water.

And still she worked, watching the damage spread in a never-ending buffet of skin and flesh. Every so often she checked Reid, placed her fingers against his neck and sought his pulse. It was weak, weakening by the second, but there wasn't much she could do.

The bullets were out.

The treatment applied.

Still the drug fought her, taunting her with what could have been. It made her realize the future was gone. Every dream she whispered to herself, the idea of mating Reid and having his cubs... Hell, she'd call them pups if it meant she got to have them.

But those fantasies were crumbling and melting into oblivion.

Evelyn poured on another pitcher, wiping away the new flow of blood that came in its wake.

No. No. No.

It wasn't lessening, it wasn't stopping, it wasn't...

She couldn't see anymore. Why couldn't she see? Did she get some of it in her eyes? Everything was blurry and he was disappearing and...

She blinked, clearing her vision.

Tears. Tears. She was crying because her future was slowly being absorbed by the floor. A sob strangled her, the pain of loss overwhelming her in a rippling wave of emotional pain and devastation. Her bear roared its objection, denying the truth that lay spread before her.

The skin on her arms rippled, the bear aching to be released so it could hunt and kill whomever injured their mate. Destroy their lives the way they'd destroyed hers. They needed to be shredded, ripped apart, and scattered across the ground.

Evelyn pressed two fingers to his neck, searching for his pulse, counting the beats and then...

One.

The seconds ticked past.

Two.

Time went on.

Three.

She willed her heart to beat for him.

"Blood." Doc Hill rasped and she spared him a glance before focusing on her mate. "They must have changed the hellfire. Made it worse for shifters."

Because she could see that the old man's injury had stopped bleeding and no longer spread. That could be the only explanation.

"Give him your blood." The doctor grunted and shifted against the wall.

"He's a wolf." Would bear blood hurt him?

"Heard he's your mate. You're built to be compatible. Species don't matter." Pain-filled eyes met hers. "What could it hurt?"

Nothing because he was dying anyway. She could see bone now, his ribs coming into view as the Carvrix delved deeper. So she let the bear come forward, let it transform her human nails to claws, and dragged one down the length of her arm. The wound sent a bolt of pain along her nerves, but she ignored it. She had a task, a purpose, and she would see it through.

Evelyn held her arm above Reid, squeezing her hand, curling and uncurling her fist to encourage blood flow. She let it rain down on his skin, and she ensured her blood fell into his wounds. It was her last chance, her last ditch effort to keep him breathing and the poison from winning.

When the cut sealed itself, she simply did it again. Over and over. The bear wanted Reid to live as much as she did, but there was no way to stop a basic biological imperative. Her body was programmed to heal.

So she bled and then healed and then she cut again.

No one stopped her. No one spoke to her. No one came near her.

Until Asher reached for Reid's neck, earning a snarl and snap from her. No one was hurting Reid. No one. And if Asher thought he could become Itan by snapping Reid's neck now, she'd make sure he didn't live past Reid's last breath.

"I'm checking his pulse, Evelyn," he lifted his hands and murmured low. "Just checking."

He didn't smell like subterfuge or hate, not like someone else in the office. Who was it? Who was happy…

"Evelyn?"

She jerked her head in a brisk nod. "Check him."

Another cut, another squeeze, another stream…

"Heartbeat is strong."

Movement to her right, the rustle of clothing and low groan told her the doctor was moving. "Wounds are healing. Time to stop, Evelyn."

Stop. Stop? But there were still…

A large hand wrapped around her wrist, stopping her from making another fist. She followed that arm to meet the owner's gaze and snarled at him—at Asher.

"It's time to stop. He won't want you killing yourself to save him. Ever."

Evelyn's throat tightened, squeezing her and cutting off her air. She wheezed as she tore her gaze from his and focused on Reid once more. "Can't lose him."

In a day he'd become necessary to her survival. Necessary. There was no living, no breathing, without him.

He was an asshole, slightly crazed, but her asshole.

"And you won't. His body will do the rest."

"I can't lose him."

"And he can't lose you. Sit back. Take care of yourself now. You lost a lot of blood."

Asher helped her—urged her—to lean against the wall while he issued orders to the other males. He organized transport for their small group. Doc Hill and Trisha would be dropped off at the human hospital to a few trusted bears. Those who would keep their eyes closed and mouths shut when it came to treatment.

You lost a lot of blood.

Evelyn didn't lose it. She knew where it went. Into the other half of her. Into Reid.

Chapter Twelve

Waking up with a warm woman in his arms wasn't the worst thing in the world. Realizing it was his mate made it a damn good thing.

Reid shifted in place, carefully lifting his head and glancing around the room. He spied a few things that belonged to him and more than a few that looked like they might be Evie's. Because he sure as hell didn't own a pile of makeup or any bras he'd decided to leave draped over the end of the bed. He drew in a lungful of air and sorted through the scents, confirming his thoughts. The space was imbued with Evie's flavors.

He was in her room. In her bed.

He lowered his head and carefully moved his legs to shift into a more comfortable position.

He was in her room. In her bed. Naked.

That was damn fine. He felt fabric against his side, telling him that Evie wore clothing, but if she was game, he could fix that. Quickly.

At least, that's what he thought until he tried to lift his arm and was assaulted with a piercing pain.

All right, he could fix it slowly.

He tried again only moaning with the move this time. "Dammit," he hissed.

What happened?

Oh. Right.

Anger at the old man, him ready to tear the dick to pieces for giving Evie a hard time, and then the familiar pop of guns.

Pop, pop, pop… He knew he took at least five bullets—he'd counted—and he remembered the scent of the human blood from Doc Hill and the receptionist. And damn, his mate was fierce when it came to digging out bullets.

He didn't have much after that. A haze of pain, the lure of sleep, his vision going fuzzy.

The pain though… He pulled that specific memory forward. It wasn't normal. He knew the feel of gunshots and it'd been… more. Stingy rather than harsh. A continuous burn with a prickly edge instead of fierce and fast.

It reminded him of one thing, one drug he'd encountered and hoped to never experience again.

The question became how'd it get to Brookfield and who mixed up that shit?

From what he remembered, it'd been something cooked up by someone in his sister's best friend's family. The relationships in Grayslake, the battles for survival, were convoluted, but it ended with discovering Carvrix and its uses. As well as who released the drug to shifter scum. Well, it seemed shifter scum had its tendrils in Brookfield too.

He shoulda expected it though. With an inner-circle and Itan like the Archers, he should have known.

Now he definitely did.

He just needed to figure out who was using it and where they'd gotten it. Then he'd kill 'em. Quick and easy.

Evie snuffled and squirmed, pressing closer to him, and her warm breath fanned his neck. She buried her face against his throat, cute nose rubbing his skin.

He'd kill 'em later. Right now he had a mate in his arms.

A delicious smelling mate. One he wanted to tease for hours. He didn't give a damn about pain or his injuries or anything happening outside the room.

Outside the room... He shot a quick look at the door, thankful it was shut. Good. No one could just walk by and peek in while he explored his mate. As much as it pissed him off to admit, he wasn't strong enough to sink into her and claim her.

But he could... taste her.

His mouth watered and cock hardened with thoughts of lapping up her cream. Of having her straddle his head and lower her pussy onto him. He'd lick and nibble, take as much as she could give and then demand more.

Nothing he liked more than eating a girl for breakfast, lunch, and dinner.

His dick throbbed, twitching as his arousal grew and anticipation increased. Shit yeah, that's what he wanted.

Reid eased over onto one shoulder, propping himself up as he nudged her to her back. She rolled easily, snuffling and whining as she drifted toward wakefulness.

He took a moment to look at her, act like some lovesick bitch, and stare at her when she wasn't awake to see what kind of pussy she'd turned him into.

That brown hair had his fingers itching to touch, that nose that sloped up at the adorable tip.

Who the hell was he to say her nose was adorable?

The thought didn't have him stopping though. He continued to her plump, bow-shaped lips that he wanted to kiss and sample.

He ignored the scarring on her face and the path they took down her neck and others across her chest. He knew pain, had his own dozens of scars on his body. She'd healed. She'd survived. She was a fighter and... all his. The rest of her body was hidden by a t-shirt and when he lifted the sheet, he realized it was one of his. Hell, one of his from the day before; sweaty and filled with his scent. She'd wanted him to surround her.

Damn he was lucky. He didn't deserve her, not after the shit he'd pulled over the years, but he'd take her anyway. Take her and run, hide, and claim her before someone else could.

But based on the aches still plaguing him, that wasn't gonna happen anytime soon. So he'd placate himself—and the wolf—with a taste.

The animal was all for that. He vaguely remembered her giving him blood. Or someone told him as he'd drifted in and out of consciousness. They'd sampled her, in a way, but he wanted her flavors on his tongue.

"Evie," he whispered her name and leaned down, nuzzling her neck. "Evie," he murmured against her skin. "Evie, wake up." He lapped at her flesh, savoring the sweetness that slid into him. Damn, she was delicious. "Evie?" She moaned and he scraped a fang along her throat before he whispered once more. "Evie, wake up."

"Hmm…" She shook her head, her hair teasing him with the move and spreading more of her scent on him. He wanted that, wanted it everywhere.

"C'mon, baby." He pressed a soft kiss to her vulnerable skin.

"Huh, Reid?" She was slightly slurred, voice groggy and filled with sleep. "You're okay?" Small hands pushed and nudged, sliding over him and the flavors of her worry and panic filled his nose. "You're awake."

He eased to his back, pretending he did it for her and refusing to acknowledge just leaning over her for that short amount of time tired him out. "I'm awake."

"Oh, God," she sobbed and propped herself up. "I thought…" She stroked his chest and rested her palm over his heart. "I mean, I knew you lived. I watched them put you in an SUV and Asher carried me and cleaned me—"

"He what?"

She froze and then she lifted her eyes from his chest and met his gaze. She glared at him, those milk chocolate eyes narrowed. "He helped me into the house and got me into the bathroom."

"No one is to touch you but me. He better not have—"

"I won't let another male put his hands on me." Her voice was soft and soothing.

He grunted. He did know. Mated females, even if they hadn't completed the mating, shied from the touch of other males. She'd endure it if necessary, but she'd always prefer her mate.

"Simone helped me. I was weak and could hardly keep my eyes open. I checked you before I crawled into bed, but I was so weak."

It was his turn to glare. "What d'ya mean, weak?"

She sighed and fell silent for so long he wondered if she'd answer. "I had to give you blood to save you."

"I… think I remember some of that, but your bear should have…"

Evie shook her head. "I gave you a lot. Almost too much. I was only half awake by the time Simone got me in bed."

"Evie…" he stroked her face, tucking her hair behind her ear. "Never do that again."

"I couldn't just let you—"

"I mean it. Me? I'm not worth hurting yourself like that." He cupped her face and ran his thumb over her cheek. "Not even a little."

"Reid, you don't understand."

"I understand that you're the most important thing to me. Can't lose you. So if the only way to keep me alive is to risk yourself, you don't do it. Me living and you dying? That shit's not happening. If there's a chance you could die trying to save me…" he shook his head. "Don't bother. Because I can't live without you and if you make me… I'll kill everything—everyone—and the only way to stop me would be a bullet to the heart. You understand me? My wolf will lose it and others will suffer. Period."

She swallowed hard, tears springing to her eyes and he hated the pain that lingered there. "I couldn't watch you die."

"And I can't live without you. You are necessary to me now. You are the reason I breathe, Evie. You get me?" He drew her closer, urging her to lower her head until he was able to brush his lips across hers. "You hear me, baby?" he murmured against her lips, breathing deeply when she released a soft sigh.

"I hear you."

"Good." He kissed her again, unable to have her close without his mouth on hers. He pressed gently, gradually drawing out what he wanted rather than demanding and taking. She needed to choose to come to him, to open and give herself to him.

Reid lapped at the seam of her lips, teasing her until she opened for him. She surrendered. And he took over, showed her that she'd mate an alpha and not some pushover. He lured her gently, beckoned her into his trap, and now he'd never release her.

Which sounded a little psycho.

He never claimed to be sane.

He slipped his tongue into her mouth, sliding past her parted lips and he gathered her flavors to him. He savored each bit of sweetness and each hint of her natural tastes. He sneaked in and out of her mouth, showing her exactly what he'd like to do. He'd slide in and out of her wet heat and pleasure her with each stroke.

That image locked in his mind, he kept his eyes closed as he made love to her with his lips. Their passion simmered, slowly heating with each passing breath, and he pulled her closer. He wanted her body aligned with his, those curves snug against him as he plundered her mouth. His cock pulsed and throbbed, aching to sink into her pussy over and over again.

He sank into the passion of their kiss, drawing in the scents that surrounded him as he lapped at her lips and gathered more of her on his tongue. Damn, if her lips were this sweet...

His dick pulsed, anxious to find out how hot and sweet her pussy would be.

And he'd get that. Soon.

He just needed her to come on his mouth first. Then, when he could breathe without being in pain, he'd fuck her. Claim her.

Mouth then dick. There, he had a plan.

One that was shot to shit when one of those hands snaked down his body. It slipped beneath the sheet that rested across his hips and then delved farther until that hot little hand encircled his shaft... then stroked him. She pumped his dick, fingers tightening as she rubbed him. Up and then down, slow and sweet and in time with the flick of her tongue.

He moaned into her mouth, enjoying the feel and taste of her. His balls ached, drawing high and tight against him as he fought off the urge to come. He wanted to fill her, bathe her in his scent until everyone knew she belonged to him and him alone.

But first he'd let her jerk him off.

His wolf—and dick, coincidentally—thought that was a fantastic idea.

Except he... had... a... plan...

Wait, she squeezed the head of his dick gently and then swiped her thumb along the slit before retreating to the base of his shaft once more.

"Shit, Evie," he gasped and arched into her hand. He ignored the aches and focused on the pleasure. She did it again, that tight fist stroking him in slow, even caresses. God, he wanted more. Wanted to come all over her hand and then watch her as she licked herself clean and...

That wasn't the plan.

Okay he'd let her jack him a little more. Just... one... more...

"Shit, baby, you gotta stop." He rushed out the words, abandoning his hold to grasp her wrist and stop her movements. "If you don't,

I'll come."

His wolf—and dick, coincidentally again—thought he was an asshole. Then he reminded the beast they were gonna taste their mate, so he was only left with a pissed off dick.

"Why?" she whimpered and just because he stopped her from stroking him didn't mean she stopped tormenting him. Nope, she still rubbed him gently with her thumb and rhythmically squeezed his shaft. Shit, that little bit was gonna send him over the edge.

Damn.

"Because," he rasped, fighting for control.

"Why?" That was a purr, like she knew what she was doing to him.

Pain in the ass.

"Because," he eased her hand from his cock and if his cock had a mouth, it would have whimpered. "The first time I come is gonna be in your pussy while you have my fangs in your shoulder. I'll claim you. But I'm not in any condition to do that. And since my dick doesn't get its way, my mouth gets what it wants."

"What about what I want?" She raised her eyebrows and he could practically see her gathering her indignation.

"My mouth wants to be on your pussy. How does your pussy feel about that?"

"Oh," her breath caught and the musky scent of her arousal drifted around him. "My pussy wants that."

Chapter Thirteen

Oh, Evelyn's pussy so wanted that. Of course, she was also self-conscious about all her curviness on his mouth like that. Not that she didn't like her shape, but her ass was big and his face and all that on him and…

And nothing. Nothing because she found herself lifted, his strong arms flexing as he forced her to straddle him, her wet pussy pressed to his stomach, which pulled a moan right past his lips.

"No panties?"

She shook her head and prayed he'd make that sound again. The vibrations from the sound traveled right to her clit in a very magical way. "I didn't have the strength. I barely got into your shirt."

His shirt that she'd refused to release once she'd found it. Her ass needed to be covered? Fine. It'd be with Reid's clothes.

"Good," he grunted. "Keeps me from having to tear your clothes apart."

"You would have—" He grasped the hem of the t-shirt and yanked, splitting it from bottom to neck. "Yes, you would have."

"Hell, yeah." His large hands slid along her thighs and then came to rest on her hips, fingers squeezing and kneading her flesh. "Now, take off that shirt and move my pussy up here."

She quirked a brow. "Your pussy?"

"Yup, it's all mine and the second I can fuck you like you deserve, I'll cover you in my scent so everyone else will know it, too."

She was listening, really, but his thumbs drew small circles over her hipbones and those tiny rotations slowly eased toward her mound. The closer he drew, the hotter she got. Her clit pulsed in time with her heart and her pussy quivered—quivered—in anticipation. She knew she wouldn't get his cock, but his mouth was a wonderful consolation prize.

Their gazes remained locked, his amber eyes boring into hers and she had no doubt her bear was equally visible to him. The animal huffed and chuffed, happy that their mate stroked and petted them. Every brush gently tugged on her skin, teasing her without touching her moist center, and she ached to have him teasing her clit. It throbbed and pulsed, her pussy growing wetter by the second and she was this close to rocking her hips against his stomach and searching for the friction she craved.

"I want you to come on my tongue."

She shuddered, body trembling with his rough words and her blood burned for him.

She slipped her arms free of the tattered remains of his shirt, leaving her entirely nude for him and he… growled, the sensual desire in his expression deepening until he was merely a man on the edge of need. His cheeks sharpened, teeth elongating and peeking past his lips. The nails on the fingers tormenting her slowly sharpened until they dug into her skin. It should have been painful. She should snap at him to be gentler, but it was so good, so right, and so perfect. That buzz of pain inflamed her, rocketing her pleasure even higher and he hadn't even touched her pussy yet.

"When we go back out there, I wanna smell you all over me." Those rumbles once again reverberated through her body, forcing her eyes to flutter closed. She rolled her hips, seeking to extend the pleasure the sounds created. "Like that?"

She moaned and nodded, eyelids drooping as she let the growing arousal sneak forward. "Yeah."

"You'll like my mouth even better." His grip changed, pressing her more firmly to his chest as he encouraged her pace to increase. "My lips and teeth on that pretty pussy."

Now she whimpered, pussy clenching and begging to be filled. "Reid."

"Ride my face, Evie. Lemme make you scream."

There was no missing the need in his gaze, the pure molten desire that filled his eyes. "Please."

The word had hardly left her lips before she was lifted once more, Reid positioning her as he desired until her knees were pressed into the mattress once more as she was astride his head, her pussy inches from his face. She squeaked and leaned forward, catching her balance by putting her palms flat on the wall.

"Perfect," he rumbled, those amber eyes now focused on the juncture of her thighs.

And he wanted her, craved her, desired her above all others. There was no missing his pure hunger.

Reid nuzzled her thigh, running his nose along her leg until he teased the outer edge of her pussy lips. "Smells s'good." He breathed deeply and released a low moan, reaffirming his words. "S'perfect."

He scraped her skin with a single fang, drawing a line on her pale flesh and sending a stinging shard down her spine to mingle with the growing arousal that assaulted her. He repeated the move, teasing her vulnerable flesh with that sharpened tip. He could destroy her or love her, tear her to shreds until she cried for mercy or give her so much pleasure she cried for more.

With the next pass, the fang was replaced by his tongue as he laved the aching scrape. Another swipe of her aching flesh followed by a third before he turned his attention to her other leg, repeating the process once more. She moaned with the renewed pain, the way it twisted and turned with the pleasure singing in her veins. Her body pulsed with her need for him, with her desperation to be touched by him.

And then… then his teasing changed, no longer tormenting her outer sex lips and focusing on the seam of her pussy. He nudged the top of her slit with his nose, breathing deeply before releasing the breath with a slow exhale. He blew warm air across her heated pussy only to suck in another lungful and release it again.

"I'll never get enough of this." She'd never get enough of him, either. "Need a taste, Evie."

His eyes flicked to her and she wasn't too proud to beg. "Please."

Reid tongued her first, sliding along her slit, up and down and up and down. She grew wetter by the second, her center clenching and aching to be consumed by him, by his mouth and someday his cock.

Evelyn forced her body to remain still, becoming a statue while he tormented her with that talented tongue. Because then… because then he slipped beyond her outer lips and with his next flick, he teased her clit.

"Oh, fuck," she trembled, body reacting to that glancing caress.

He moaned and repeated the move, the delicate torment yanking a groan from her mouth. Then it became a rhythmic series of flicks and taps. She moaned and cried out with each one, urging him to go harder, faster, more.

He sucked and nibbled her clit then, taking what he wanted as he sampled her while still giving her pleasure. He gripped her hips, holding her steady and moving her as he desired. He eased her back to torment her clit and forced her hips forward when he wanted to dip his tongue into her pussy. He lapped at her very center, teasing her opening with his agile tongue until she was desperate to be filled by him, to be taken and branded by Reid.

"Please, oh God. Please, Reid."

He just moaned and continued in his attentions.

Lick. Suck. Nibble.

Over and over he teased her—tormented her.

And she wanted more. More of him, more of his mouth, his hands, his body. She craved his touch like a drug and lost herself to the ecstasy he created.

Him, the werewolf Itan that everyone called deadly, gave her nothing but bliss.

He gave her even more when his fingertips ghosted over her ass and teased her crack, dipping between her cheeks to find her hidden entrance.

"Reid. I…" She hadn't ever been taken there, been touched there, but with him… she wanted it all.

So she didn't stop him, she took his forbidden attentions, torn between the pleasure of his mouth and the dark ecstasy of his fingers. She rode both edges, seeking her bliss with the two separate sensations until she couldn't tell one torment from the next. Her body simply knew joy. It knew what it craved and what it sought, so she allowed the sensations to drug her. She moaned with each nibble, groaned with each lick, and gasped when the tip of his finger slipped into her ass.

"Reid!"

He simply moaned, taking more from her and giving just as much in return. Each passing second pushed her higher, shoved her closer to release until she knew it would overcome her at any second.

"Reid, gonna… come…" She wasn't sure what she was saying anymore, just that the sensations slowly overrode her every thought and she was nothing more than a body of sensation that seemed electrified by the pleasure filling her veins.

But he knew. He knew and pleasured her even further. He moaned against her pussy, growling and groaning while his finger pushed even deeper into her ass. And she loved it, loved every inch deeper he slid, loved the forbidden penetration until she ached to have his cock fill her there, too.

Her nerves sizzled with need, the precipice in sight and dragging her nearer with each breath, with every heartbeat, and every thought. Her nipples were hard and aching along with her pussy, body ready for the ultimate release.

Soon. Soon. Soon.

The pleasure didn't just fill her, it consumed her, overriding every thought as it increased. A bubble of ecstasy surrounded her, wrapping her in a sphere of impending bliss until each breath brought another trembling wave of joy.

"Reid…" It was there, right on the edge, pussy clenching and aching to be filled while it tightened around air. Her clit throbbed in time with those milking ripples until wave after wave of joy trembled through her body. "Please…"

She needed a little more, a little something that would send—

Reid scraped a single fang across her clit, the sharp tooth scratching the bundle of nerves and it sent her flying into the air, over the edge and beyond. She came with his name on her lips, the ecstasy stealing her control as she trembled and gasped with the overwhelming sensations. Her body was no longer her own, the bliss forcing her toes to curl and muscles to twitch without thought.

And he didn't stop. He continued to fuck her ass, mouth working her clit, while she dealt with the consuming pleasure that seemed to go on and on. The waves continued, rising and falling in a drugging ebb and flow of ecstasy that she could easily become addicted to. His attentions gradually slowed, bringing her down from the extreme heights of joy until her heart slowed to its normal rhythm and her breaths no longer came in heaving gasps as she fought for air.

Evelyn leaned forward, forehead to the wall as her strength fled and the drowsy after-sex glow overtook her. That was also about the time she realized she must have gotten claws at some point because they were now deeply embedded in the drywall. Damn.

Reid moaned, drawing her attention once more, his lips now brushing gentle kisses to her mound and then finally giving her leg one last nuzzling. That's when his gaze collided with hers with a low hum. "Delicious."

"Yeah?" She gave him a small, lazy grin.

"Hell, yeah. If my dick isn't in your pussy you can bet my mouth will be teasing this pretty clit of yours."

She liked the sound of that. It was crass, sure, but oh so good. "Okay."

More than okay.

"Good," he grunted. "Now come lay down. You were hurt too."

Now he remembered.

But she didn't care about how long it took him to realize she'd been injured as well because the orgasm and then his snuggles more than made up for her new exhaustion.

Evelyn eased close, draping half her body across his with a soft sigh. "This good?"

He grunted. She took that as a yes.

* * *

Reid held her close, her chest to his side, draped across him like a lush blanket. He absorbed her heat, reveled in their closeness, and the softness of her skin. This was what he'd missed in his life.

Not sex. He'd fucked his way through his old pack in Redby and half the female bears at Terrence's compound. But he always kicked the bitches out after or left if he'd gone to their place. Come and done.

Now? Now his wolf howled at him, telling him that if he even thought about leaving, it'd kick his ass. The beast agreed that the first time he came with Evie would be when he was buried deeply inside her. It went on to tell him that hard-on or not, his ass was staying put. He could suffer.

His animal was an asshole.

But when he ran his fingers along her smooth back, fingers dancing over her silken skin, he figured suffering through blue balls was worth it. Her small hand stroked his chest, fingers drawing random lines on his skin. Each twirl and swirl had her traveling farther south, edging toward the sheet that draped across his hips. When she went to delve beneath the fabric, he grasped her wrist, stopping her.

"No, Evie."

"Reid," she whined. "I wanna make you feel good."

He nuzzled her head, drawing in her scent with each inhale. "Holding you makes me feel good. Touching you like this." He shook his head. "You have no idea what this does for me."

"You're not gonna let me…"

Reid smiled and pressed a soft kiss to her head. The scent of her arousal still surrounded him, her musky essence teasing his wolf, and it tried to wheedle a claiming out of him. If only the Carvrix hadn't done such a good job. His shifter blood would have healed a normal injury by now, but with that poison… not so much.

"No, I'm not." He gave her a gentle squeeze. "Evie, this is a gift. Right here. Right now. I've never had this and right now, that's enough."

Her hand traveled back to his chest, fingers ghosting over his abs and then finally settling over his heart once more. "You've never stuck around after sex?"

Her voice was teasing, but she had no idea how deep his feelings went. "I've never enjoyed comfort like this. Not just sex, but any of it."

She stilled and he cursed himself, knowing those few words opened up a can of pain that he didn't want to open.

"What do you mean?"

"It's not important." Today, anyway. Hopefully not ever. He didn't want to go back there. To that time when his life was shaped and formed through blood and pain.

Evie wasn't going to let him get away with it, though. "I think it is." She lifted her head, turning it so she could prop her chin on his chest. Their gazes met, and he knew what she was gonna say before the words left her mouth. "Tell me."

And because she was his mate, he couldn't not tell her.

Reid closed his eyes, unwilling to see any disgust or hatred that might fill her expression. Why shouldn't she be disgusted? Or why wouldn't she hate him for what he'd done over the years?

"It's hard to find one thing." He sought his memories, ignoring the pain that came with 'em and instead separated himself from the emotional hurts. Him with emotions? Yeah. He had 'em. He just didn't let them come out to play very often.

"Tell me anything."

Anything. "You know, I…" God, was he going to admit his fears? His heartache? His pain? For Evie, he would. There had to be more to them than fucking. "The first time I saw my mom beaten I was three. Shit, I remember that day."

He remembered it all right. He could still taste his mother's blood on his tongue, the gashes that marred her skin.

Evie gave him time to gather his thoughts and he was thankful she did. "My parents were true mates, but there's always been something different about my father when you compare him to others. He had that edge that made him just a little stronger, just a little meaner than everyone else. Which was what made him a good alpha."

Reid watched more than one dominance fight that ended with death for his father's opponent. "But the mean…" he sighed. "I can't explain it. Saying my father was a mean sonofabitch just isn't enough." He flipped through his past, trying to find something other than the lesson he'd learned at three. He decided it'd been a mistake to start there. He should—

"Tell me what happened to your mom."

It was a mistake. "I skinned my knee." Out tumbling with the neighborhood kids. He hadn't grown into his asshole genes yet. Still a kid having fun, running and tussling with the other wolves. "I didn't cry, Bennetts don't cry. We're not pussy assed bitches." See, Pops, I remember. "But one of the kids, boy destined to be our omega, he was so small and timid unless we were playing." He wasn't gonna think about what happened to Adam. "We got tangled and went down, both of us cut up. It was just a kid thing. Playing and falling, me landing on the bottom and Adam on top."

Reid knew that'd been something else that enraged his father. The fact that Adam had appeared to dominate Reid. They'd been three, but already he was being groomed for the alpha position.

"Adam was crying which made me get teary and our mothers came running over to brush us off and offer us comfort. It was so stupid. It was what kids do."

He closed his eyes, letting history creep forward. Letting himself remember the scent of the grass and the gravel that dug into his knees. It'd burned and cut his skin, but he wasn't gonna cry because babies cried and Reid wasn't a baby. He was an alpha.

So instead of being a baby, he told Adam it was all gonna be okay. He didn't need to cry. And when Adam realized he'd hit the alpha's son, he'd cried harder. It was the first time he'd smelled fear from another kid, or had one run from him. Adam crawled his momma like she was a tree and hid his face in her neck. He kept on crying and apologizing.

I'm sorry, I'm sorry, I'm sorry…

Reid didn't care. He just hoped it'd scar. Scars were cool.

"My mother told him it was okay. That everything was fine. There was no reason to be upset." He snorted. "God, with my father there was every reason." He shook his head. "He came home after dark, bone tired from work and hungry. I'd already eaten so I was playing in the living room. Don't even remember what was on the TV now." It'd been important back then, though. "My parents were in the kitchen, talking about whatever adults discussed and then my father called for me. And when he called, you went. There was none of that begging some parents do. He said your name and your ass did whatever he said."

He learned that by watching others in the pack, the way his dad reacted when they took their time.

"I scrambled into the kitchen, racing to get to the table and stared at him, waiting to see what he wanted. And he… just stared. Stared at me until I remembered I was supposed to look down." He ran his fingers along Evie's arm, reminding himself he had her by his side. "Even at three I didn't feel like I needed to submit. It just never occurred to me. When I challenged him and won twenty years later, I knew why. I was stronger than him even then. Perhaps not in body, but heart."

It wasn't something he'd acknowledged until that moment and it shifted a few things inside him, altered his view just enough to make the world seem different. Just enough to…

"What happened next?"

"Right. Next." Next he'd questioned Reid. Over and over. What happened? Who hit who? Did he cry? Are you sure that's what happened? "He had me tell him what happened. I wanted to look to my mom, to see her smile and know that everything was okay because he smelled more than mad. It was rage, but then, I'd never scented it before." Years later after his mother had been raped and beaten by a pack of hyenas, he'd experienced it again. "And when I was done he didn't say a damned thing. Not one. And I was squirming because I wasn't sure if I'd made my alpha happy or not so I stole a peek. I lifted my eyes and saw my father staring at my mother, and she had tears on her cheeks and then…"

You lying cunt.

"He backhanded her. One hit sent her sprawling across the floor and by the time she stopped sliding, blood poured from her split cheek." He'd never scented his mother's blood before. Never caught a hint of those flavors, but he'd never forget them. Not ever. "I ran to her. She was my mother and I was idealistic. No one hurt mothers. You just didn't. I ran as fast as my legs could carry me, crying for her, but I never made it. My father caught me with his boot. Sent me flying through the air and I didn't stop until I slammed against the wall." He brushed a kiss across her forehead. "It hurt like hell. I think that day was the most painful of my life and it had nothing to do with hitting a wall."

And everything to do with watching his dad beat his mom until she was a broken, bloody heap.

"When he was done he came over to me. Told me it was my fault."

"Reid…" her whisper tried to pull him from the past, but it was no use. He had to get it out.

"I let a pussy boy dominate me and if I'd been a stronger wolf he wouldn't have had to listen to Adam's dad boast about his kid beating me. Then my mom lied to protect me. I had to be a man—a better wolf—or I'd end up like her." Bloody. Broken. Beaten.

"That's…"

"Fucked up. But it meant that the next time I saw Adam, I put him down hard. That any time someone tried to disrespect me, I went after them. What I wanted, I took. You're strong or you're not. It's yours or it's not. He raised me in a world of black and white. Terrence and Clary are trying to teach me there are shades of gray, but it's hard to break the cycle."

Really hard.

"I can't believe he did that to you. Where's your mom now?"

"Gone." It was hard to keep the agony out of his voice. "She'd lived through a lot of shit. So much… The hyenas kidnapped, raped, and beat her when I was six. When Dad found out she was pregnant from it, she was sent away and gave birth to my sister, Zoey. Then she came back alone."

"Oh, God. He made her leave your sister behind?" Tears clogged his mate's throat and he hated that his past brought her pain.

"Yeah." Left her behind with a screwed up wolf pack. "Yeah, he did. And so, when I thought I could take him, when I was sure the time was right, I talked to my mom. Warned her. No one should have to learn that their mate is gonna die right before he takes his last breath. And I was gonna kill him. But he found out somehow.

"Someone overheard us talking and before I could challenge him, she was accused of betraying her mating to him and he had the right to kill her." Reid had heard plenty of bones breaking over the years. His own during a shift or others when he killed them. But the snap of her neck… he'd never forget that. "He was dead within fifteen minutes."

The best fifteen minutes of his life. He didn't glory in the kill today, but then… he'd bathed in his father's blood and loved every second of it.

A timid knock on the bedroom door came just before a voice called through the wood. "Reid?"

Reid sighed. It looked like their time alone was up.

"Reid?" Her voice was a soft whisper.

He looked down at her, eyebrow raised. "Yeah, baby?"

"It wasn't your fault. What he did to your mom, it wasn't."

"Okay." He didn't believe that but he'd humor her.

"And I'm glad he's dead. I'm glad you killed him. I hope you made it painful."

"I did." Reid's fingers tingled and nails ached as his wolf remembered the way his father's skin split so beautifully for his claws. "I did."

Chapter Fourteen

They didn't have any choice but to leave the privacy of Evie's room. Their small cocoon gave them a reprieve from the drama outside the space, but it'd have to be faced at some point. There were plans to be made, digging to be done.

Carvrix in Brookfield? By accident or design?

Who knew. But he would before all was said and done.

He twined his fingers with Evie's, drawing her down the hallway as he headed toward the living room. The low murmur of voices reached him, men and women softly talking in the center of the house. From what he heard, there were at least a dozen bears—men and women—waiting on them. Maybe more. He found the most tormented females tended to stay silent and he hoped they'd find their voice someday.

"Hey, Reid." Owen called out to him, but for one more second he ignored the Grayslake bear. This was more important.

He kept moving through the den, letting his gaze touch on each shifter in the house. Shifters didn't need to be touched or spoken to in order feel acknowledged. A look was all it took. A meeting of eyes.

I see you. You're important to me. You're mine.

And they all were important even if he got glares in return. Reid knew from experience that one stare could mean the difference between insurrection and peace. He'd taken out his father, hadn't he? When his dad was busy beating—

"Hey, Reid." He yanked his mind from that path and to the bear still trying to get his attention, to the hand now gripping Reid's forearm.

Reid had played well with others for days. Days. Longer than he had in… forever. For some reason, this asshole—even if he was from Grayslake and knew Reid's history—forgot who he was, where he came from, and how that'd shaped him. He spun, hand splayed and in one swift move he had his fingers wrapped around his throat and back against the wall. Could he hurt him? Yes. Had he? Not yet. It was all about surprise, intimidation. Based on his wide eyes and gaping mouth, Reid was successful.

"Never," he purred and leaned close, "ever, disrespect me in front of the clan. I am the Itan. You want my notice, you ask for it and you wait. You don't put your hands on me like I'm some child who can't pay attention to the world around me. You are here at my request and mine alone. Your mother may have put you on this earth, but I will take you out of it." The roll of their fear stroked his back, a hint of panic teasing the edge and he battled against his beast. It didn't just hate disrespect, he loathed it. He tightened his grip, making Owen wheeze, and he leaned forward to whisper in the bear's ear. "Do we have an understanding?"

"The," Owen gasped, "the Southeast Itan sent me. You have no right—"

"I have every right. As I said, my request brought your here since—as a trained EMT—you're the closest thing to a Healer we have." Sure, Evie was trained, but he didn't want her five feet from his side, let alone meeting with other bears. "You're to meet with the clan and make yourself available to them at their convenience. You don't chase them. You don't hound them. You sit in your office and leave your door open. You show them respect and consideration while you listen and care for them. You tell me if there's something I can do to make this shit better."

"That violates patient-doctor—"

He squeezed a little harder, feeling the rage and adrenaline sink into his blood. Yeah, Owen had forgotten who he dealt with. Reid was better than he'd been when he joined the bears, but even after going through eight therapists, he was still a crazy fuck.

"We both understand that a smart bear—any shifter—has reason to be afraid of me. So you're gonna be the closest thing they have to a doctor and clan member liaison in one until I get my inner-circle set." He kept his hand in place and slowly turned his gaze on the cluster of women in the living room and then to some of the other bears who called Brookfield home. "None of you have come to me with shit, so I'm telling you to go to Owen. Despite his current idiocy, he's a smart and caring bear. There will be no repercussions if you bring a grievance to Owen. He knows enough to bring shit to my door that needs to be addressed. You tell him not to say something, and he won't."

He focused on Katherine and then the female beside her. Then the one next to her. He kept going around the circle, telling them with his eyes that they should give him their trust.

I will protect you. I will care for you. You are mine.

Katherine was the first to nod, her expression clouded with fear and hope.

The others fell in line and their acceptance slowly traveled around the room.

"Good. We're having a gathering tonight to rid the clan of the evil it's harbored. You have any grievances between now and then, you go to Owen. You come to me."

Evie's scent hit him a split second before she stepped into his sight, his shirt hanging from her body and their mixed scent clung to her skin. "Or me." His mate shot a glare at Owen. "Or you can come to me."

"You..." Gasp. "Can't just..." Wheeze. "Order me—"

"Amazingly enough," Reid drawled, "I can."

And because the wolf wanted to, he squeezed a little tighter, enjoyed the darkening of Owen's face as it reddened and then purpled. The animal liked it, liked the wave of fear that came from Owen as he continued to steal his air.

"Reid?" There was no worry or concern in his mate's tone. Simple curiosity.

Another subtle squeeze, pulling that last whiff of air from Owen's lungs, and then he released the bear. Owen fell to the ground with a gasp, fighting to fill his lungs with air, and Owen shot him a glare.

"Want it again?" His wolf pushed forward and released a growl.

The bear dropped his gaze in an instant, face paling until it nearly blended with the white on the walls. "Sorry," he whispered.

He grunted and turned his attention back to the room at large. "What I said stands. You can't talk to me, you go to Owen or Evelyn," his Evie whimpered and a glance showed her confusion. He reached out and gave her hand a gentle squeeze. She was Evelyn to them, Evie to him. It was a clear difference he'd explain later. Never did he want to hear Evie fall from anyone's lips. "There's also Asher. He's my Enforcer. I'll establish the rest of the hierarchy over the next few days, but this is the infrastructure as it stands today."

Reid's gaze shifted over everyone once more. "I want you to understand something. I know your fear. I know what lives in your hearts and that you've fought to just survive over the years." The tension ratcheted up and he'd never hated the reputation he'd cultivated more. "But there are two things you don't know that you should.

"I demand respect and submission--my wolf allows nothing less. I also claim this clan as mine. I will protect you until my last breath and I will kill anyone—anyone—who threatens my bears and this town. Today's attack will not go unpunished. I will cut them. I will claw them. I will rip off pieces of flesh and I will gut them while they still breathe.

"A crazy male kills to kill. I kill so others understand it would be crazy to touch what belongs to me." The fear remained high, but he felt some of it ease with his words. "I will kill for you. I will die for you. Because you are mine."

The panic slowly ebbed, the Brookfield men and women calming with his declaration. Asher was unmoved, simply raising a single brow as if it say, "You done now?" and Reid nodded. He was done. He'd said what needed saying and now he'd take a few minutes to breathe, to just be with Evie. They'd loved on one another—he could still taste her on his tongue—but they hadn't talked, hadn't simply enjoyed the world around them.

Meeting Brookfield bears and laughing with her all afternoon was one thing, but he needed more.

And wasn't that a pussy-whipped thought. He was a chick that needed to connect with his mate.

What happened to him?

He tugged on Evie, drawing her toward the back door and leaving silence in their wake. Hope grew that they'd escape without being stopped, but that fell flat the moment Carter neared.

"Itan?" his gaze remained lowered, but there was no hint of terror clinging to him.

"Yeah," he kept the growl from his voice. Barely.

"Do you think leaving the house is safe?"

Probably not.

"I don't imagine it is, but being in a doctor's office in town wasn't either. So I'll take my chances. If someone wants to be a pussy and take me out with a bullet, they'll do it."

The bear's eyes flicked to his and there was no missing the glare. A glare, but only a little fear. Well, at least his speech reassured someone. Or it could be that Carter was involved in saving his sorry ass. "With all due respect, Itan, I'm trusting you to deliver on your promises, which means I don't want to lose an Itan who could help this clan heal."

Reid grinned and looked to Evie. "He likes me a little bit."

That had his mate snorting. "Reid, give him a break."

He wanted to give Carter shit, but then he remembered the pain the clan endured for who knew how long. So instead of teasing, he reached for the male. He wrapped his hand around the back of Carter's neck and squeezed, bringing the bear forward until the male's bowed head rested against Reid's shoulder. Wolves thrived on contact, on feeling the dominance first hand to connect with their alpha and take comfort in the stronger wolf's presence. So that's what he gave the bear. Nothing sexual, nothing that would make a mate jealous. Just a touch to tell him he wasn't alone. Like a parent to a child, he reassured Carter.

"I'm good. Trust your Itan. Know that my mate and this clan are the two most important things in my life. We're walking out to the gathering clearing before I call everyone together tonight. If you feel the need to protect me, you send out a few armed bears and they stay back. You got me?"

Carter shuddered and Reid knew his instincts were right. Bear or wolf, the connection was needed. "Yes, Itan."

Apprehension still followed them out the door, but the overwhelming fear was gone. It was a step. Good or bad, it was a step. He just hoped it was in the right direction. Was it subterfuge? One of the bears pretending to be a friend, sneaking into the den under the guise of need, while plotting his death. Because Evie might not remember, or be willing to acknowledge it, but as he lay dying on that worn carpet, he heard six words that told him someone who was supposed to protect him was out to kill him.

No one else was supposed to get hurt.

Chapter Fifteen

Evelyn stayed at his side, quietly moving through the forest with her hand in his. They didn't speak, not as they crossed the wide lawn and not as they crossed the tree line. It wasn't until the foliage masked their location that he spoke. Or rather, moved.

In one fluid spin, he had her pinned to the trunk of a tree, his mouth on hers as he plundered her depths. His tongue delved into her, licking and caressing hers with a sensual rhythm that had her desire flaring to life once more. She'd just come on his mouth and she wanted him again. She ached for his mouth, his fingers, his… cock. God, she wanted his cock. Deep and hard, but she swallowed her pleas.

They'd mate, but not while a half-dozen bears traipsed after them. And it was at least a half-dozen of Grayslake and Brookfield's finest. At least, she recognized one scent, perhaps two, as belonging to the town.

She pulled her lips from his and forced her lids to part. Panting, she forced words from her mouth. "Is that a good idea?"

"Kissing you? Yes." He leaned down once more but a hand on his chest stopped him.

"No, I mean, the Brookfield bears following us."

Reid grinned. "You like me a little bit, too."

Evelyn rolled her eyes. "More than a little. Which is why I don't want you shot or mauled by two of our own."

"How much more?" The need, the craving, for the truth lived in his eyes. As did hope and she ached for him. The story he'd told... what he'd endured...

"A lot, Reid. More than I should in so short a time, but I can't help it. You're..."

"Your mate. And you're mine. I don't just like you a lot, Evie. I told you, you're necessary to me, to my survival. You are my other half and if I don't have you, I have no reason to breathe."

She nodded. What else could she do? Her feelings drew closer and closer to his with every minute they spent together. Was it fast? Yes, but most shifter matings were. Biologically, their bodies were drawn together, but emotionally... their past bound them. Evelyn's emotional wounds were fresh and raw, while Reid's were deep in his marrow and long lasting.

He lowered his head and pressed his forehead to hers. "And if it wasn't for these wounds on my back, I'd claim you right this second. The asshole who did this is dead. Not just because he attacked me, but because you were put at risk and it delayed our mating."

"Do you think we should be doing this then? Shouldn't we be tracking him or something?"

That had him pulling back with a grin and she immediately missed his closeness. "Asher has that under control."

"How do you know?" They'd been together and he hadn't time to speak with Asher alone since they'd woken.

"Because that's what a good Enforcer does. He protects the hell out of his Itan. That includes finding the asshole who hurt me. Then, once he's found, I get the joy of cutting him into tiny pieces."

Evelyn grinned and rolled her eyes. "You and your killing."

Reid's breath caught and he froze in place, staring at her. A vulnerability she'd never seen filled his expression. "Do you have a problem with that part of me? I can't change who I am, but I can—"

She placed a hand on his cheek. "I like who you are." She quirked her lips in a half-smile. "I told the women that everyone's a little crazy, you just don't hide yours." Then she shook her head. "But I don't think that's it. Our pasts shape us, but you…" She met his gaze, unflinching as they stared at one another. Owen was nearly choked for staring at Reid, but her mate simply gave her a curious expression. His beast was nowhere in sight. It was all man. All her man. "You're black and white, Reid. I see you as very Old Testament. Eye for an eye with a few extra shades of red."

Of course, he snorted. "If that's what ya wanna believe."

"It's the truth."

"We'll agree to disagree."

But she knew she was right, even if no one else could see what she saw. So instead of arguing about it, she slipped away and darted down the path. "C'mon. You wanna check things out, so let's check 'em out."

He groaned and turned, following her with his gaze. "Can't I get a few more kisses out of you?"

"You gonna finish?"

"I can't." He glared at her and it did absolutely nothing.

"Then I'm gonna have to say no. I can only deal with you being a pussy-tease for so long before I can't promise I won't throw you down and take what I want."

That had him smiling, eyes holding a sensual heat she'd come to recognize. "Baby, you can throw me anywhere. Use me any way you see fit."

And damn but she wanted to use him. All of him and all at once.

Except now wasn't the time and the middle of the woods while someone wanted to kill Reid wasn't the place. Dammit.

"Let's go, sexy." She tilted her head to the side and jerked her chin. "The clearing's this way." After that, she bolted. She darted toward the clearing, trusting Reid and his bears to keep them safe as she raced down the path.

Her mate followed her, a low growl preceding his rapid pursuit. She crushed dried leaves and twigs beneath her feet, not even bothering to keep quiet as she fled. Reid's steps were just as noisy, his large boots crunching and snapping everything in his path, his grumbles accompanying every stomp. It was those low words and half-assed snarls that had her laughing, his growls that had her giggling, and the near roars that had her outright laughing.

She ducked and darted, climbing a tree and launching herself from one to another before dropping back to the ground thirty feet away and to the right of the pathway. She may have more curves than the average bear, but that never, ever stopped her from being just as fast, fierce, and stealthy—when she wanted to be—as the other bears.

She just looked better doing it.

The clearing came into sight, the break in the trees easily seen as the sunlight beckoned her forward, and she increased her speed. She pushed harder, went faster, and raced to her goal. Only to be... tackled just before she stepped into the wide swath of land. Large arms wrapped around her and legs restrained hers as they rolled. Not once did her skin scrape the grass or rocks dig into her flesh. Not once did her head bounced on the hard earth.

Because of him.

Reid may have tackled her, but he kept her safe at the same time, rolling them across the ground without allowing her to be injured until they finally came to a stop twenty feet from the tree line.

"Got you." He hovered over her, his weight now balanced on his legs and elbows as he kept her caged. "I'll always catch you."

"When I want to be caught."

"Nah, I'll always find you. There's nothing you—or anyone else—could do to keep you from me. The wolf knows your taste now, knows your pure scent and the sound of your voice. Above all, it knows you belong to us. You try to leave and he'll hunt you."

She raised her eyebrows. "That's sweet. And creepy. You understand how others could think that's creepy."

Then… he laughed. The sound breaking free of his lips in a rush. It wasn't the cocky chuckle or fake huff that he gave others. It was an honest to God laugh. And it was beautiful.

Joy filled her, the knowledge that she'd done that for him, she'd helped him break free of the constant rage and got him to laugh for real. It was a heady feeling. And sexy. Damn, it was so sexy. Her pussy responded to his nearness, his overwhelming scent and the feel of his chest against hers. Musk and man sank into her lungs, imbuing her with his flavors and she could do nothing but draw more into her lungs. More and more and more again. Her nipples pebbled, her inner-bear lumbering to her feet and nudging her to do something about her desire, her need.

Well, what the hell did the bear expect? The middle of the gathering clearing with bears on their tail and Reid injured wasn't exactly the place to cue up Marvin Gaye and sing Let's Get it On.

It told her it absolutely was the perfect place.

Horny bear.

It agreed.

Being tasted was one thing. Tasting him was another. Which seemed like the most perfect, magical idea ever.

Mouth watering, Evelyn couldn't find it in herself to disagree.

She wiggled, needing to sate the growing ache between her legs, and was gratified when he hardened against her hip. She knew he was long and thick, his girth easily able to stretch and fill her exactly how she liked. He'd fill her pussy soon, but for now she'd sate her arousal with him filling her mouth.

"Evie," he growled in warning.

She didn't care. She wanted him, wanted more of what they'd started in the house before the past threw a pall over their passion and reality intruded and destroyed their moment. There would be no knocking or murmured conversations to distract them now.

"What?" She opened her eyes wide, doing her best to appear

innocent as she rolled her hips and caressed his cloth-covered dick.

"Don't."

"Is that a real don't or a half don't."

Reid groaned and buried his face in her hair. "Evie," he rasped.

"Reid," she whispered, putting every hint of her desire into the single word.

"We're supposed to be…"

"Spending time together away from the house. Exploring the gathering clearing." She wiggled once more. "I think we've done enough exploring, don't you?"

"Evelyn."

"Saying my name over and over won't change the fact that I want you." She turned her head and nipped his ear. "I want you in my mouth, Reid. You stopped me before, but I still want it."

"You're gonna kill me," he moaned and tightened his hold. He rolled them until she was on top, Reid spread out before her. "But I'm pretty sure it'll be worth it."

She winked at him. "Hell yeah, it will. I give the best blow jobs this side of the—"

His rumbling growl silenced her. "Never, ever talk about sex and others."

"I didn't mention—"

"Ever, Evie. I don't wanna know why you think you give the best blow jobs because that means you'd given them to others. I find out their names and I'll have to kill 'em. I can't fuck you and kill them at the same time, so save a few assholes and don't say it again."

"You're jealous." And she liked it.

"I'm possessive and have a damn good imagination. As far as I'm concerned, you're a virgin."

"Fine," she eased down his body, crawling backward until the large bulge in his jeans was at eye level. "I'm pure as snow." She stared at his hidden length and licked her lips. "And I want a taste." She flicked her attention to his. "Please?"

"Baby, you never have to ask. You want my dick?" She nodded and he placed his hands behind his head. "Then take it."

One flick of a button and tug on a zipper allowed her to tug his jeans down and release his cock. Then she did exactly as she desired even if some of their bears lingered in the woods out of sight.

Evelyn took it.

Chapter Sixteen

Oh, fuck, she took it. Evelyn's plump lips wrapped around the head of his cock as if she was made for him and him alone. He hadn't chased her, hadn't raced outside and through the forest, expecting it to end up with his jeans down and dick out.

Couldn't say he was sorry about it though. Just unexpected. He'd intended to spend some time with her, get to know her and shit. Do those things couples did before they mated.

Then again, he assumed most couple did the regular old sniff and bang.

If they hadn't gotten hurt…

That thought kinda disappeared when she sucked his dick like a vacuum cleaner. She slid down his shaft, that tongue tapping the underside of his length as she swallowed more and more of him. His wolf howled in joy, its appreciation of their new situation thrumming through his inner-beast.

Reid was just happy to have his dick sucked.

She hummed, sliding lower and lower until the head of his cock nudged the back of her throat. Then she hummed. Mother. Fucking. Hummed. The vibrations had him moaning and rocking his hips and he fought the urge to push deep, make her take all of him.

"Evie," he whispered, his voice hoarse with his need for her. "Fuck."

Evie whimpered and slowly retreated, revealing his slick cock inch by inch until she reached the tip once more. Then she met his gaze. Met his gaze while she stroked his shaft and sucked his cock head. That talented tongue teased him, circling then tapping then there was sucking and holy hell her fang teased his slit.

"Shit, baby." He wasn't sure what he was trying to say, but the sting of pain that came from that move had him moaning and groaning, aching to pull away and push closer.

Who wanted teeth by their dick?

Him, apparently.

Because when she swallowed him once more, he whimpered at the loss of that sting.

She set up a slow rhythm then, sliding up and down his cock, her hand working in tandem with her mouth. She sucked and teased, nibbled and tormented. And all the while he kept his gaze trained on her. He propped his weight on his elbows and just watched his mate suck his dick. There was nothing more intimate. Nothing that showed trust like this act. She didn't have him by the balls, she had him by the dick.

And he hoped she never gave it up.

On her next rise, she removed her mouth entirely, hand still squeezing and sliding along his shaft but her mouth was free. "I want you to come in my mouth."

"You can't say—" She squeezed the base of his length and he groaned, trying to remember what he was trying to tell her, but it didn't seem important when she swallowed him again.

He lost himself to the pleasure, to the joy of being inside her this much. He'd pound her hard later. He was gonna come in her now. Because he wanted that, wanted to paint her with his scent from inside out and... fuck, fuck, fuck she cupped his balls, giving them a gentle squeeze and soft roll.

"Shit, Evie. Don't..."

Stop. He didn't want her to stop. Ever.

And she didn't. It was if she understood him, knew what he was saying even if the words didn't leave his lips.

Her pace increased, the soft slurp of her mouth on his cock joining his moans... and hers. There was no missing her scent in the air, the flavors that told him she enjoyed sucking his cock. She rose and fell, taking him deep before letting him slid free only to be swallowed once more. Up and down, over and over...

Reid's cock pulsed, twitching and jerking with the pleasure that coursed through him. With every beat of his heart, the sensations grew, expanding and exploding to fill him completely. She teased his balls and tormented his dick, ratcheting his bliss even higher and his release neared, edging closer and closer with each of her sounds. His balls were hard and tight against him, body preparing for the ultimate ecstasy the longer she teased him.

"God, Evie. It's... Gonna..." It's heaven and hell and he was gonna come any second.

That had his mate whimpering and sucking harder, moving faster, and he couldn't stop the subtle flex of his hips each time she took in more of him. Each swallow, each tap of her tongue and each rise and fall shoved him toward his orgasm. He welcomed it with open arms, his wolf howling once more at the joy his mate gave them. It yipped in happiness and he wished the asshole would shut up because any second now...

Oh shit, her finger snaked behind his balls and rubbed that small patch of skin before going farther and tapping his puckered entrance. She caressed and teased and oh damn...

His breath caught, body suspended between heaven and hell and then heaven won as she pressed firmly against his unforgiving flesh. He came, back arched, mouth open as a howl escaped his lips and he released the sound, sending it echoing through the forest.

His dick twitched and jerked with each spurt of cum that erupted from the tip and filled her mouth and Evie... swallowed. Her throat worked against the head of his cock, her lips buried in his cropped curls as she took more and more from him. The pleasure that came from the act overwhelmed him, stealing any semblance of control and he fisted her hair, holding her steady as he filled her over and over again. The ecstasy of his release rolled through him, attacking him from all sides as it burned his nerves and enveloped him in a blissful blanket of satisfaction.

It continued with every suck, with every whimper and every groan until he felt himself softening, sensed his dick growing lax inside her mouth and he finally tore his fingers from her hair. But she didn't pull away immediately. No, she kept him inside her mouth, those lips remaining around his shaft until he was fully sated. She slowly released him, letting him gently fall from her lips until he was fully bared to the hot, humid air. She gave his cock one last, chaste kiss and his dick twitched in response, body trying to respond to her nearness once more.

If his dick hadn't just been sucked like a champion…

Reid gave her a soft, lazy smile. Sated from her attentions. "Baby, that was—"

But Evie wasn't looking at him. Nope, her attention was over his shoulder as she scrambled away from him. Wolf didn't like that one bit. In fact, it growled and grumbled and was really pissed that she tried to leave him immediately after giving him the best blowjob of his life.

"Oh, shit, Reid." She pointed at something behind him and he immediately flipped, shoving Evie from his legs as he leapt to his feet. He tugged his jeans up as he moved, pulling them back to his hips as he faced whatever—whoever—scared his mate. And if it was one of his own bears ruining his post-orgasm buzz… they were dead.

And yeah, he figured it was okay to kill this bear. "Gary." The male narrowed his eyes, the irises going black the longer he glared at Reid. "What was your plan here?"

Gary cocked the revolver, the hammer easing back and making that click so many recognized. Instead of being afraid, he was curious. A six-shooter to take out a wolf? Maybe he thought he'd get a lucky shot? Reid would have come with at least a Glock. Fifteen rounds plus one in the chamber. Facing a bear? He would have brought and extra mag.

The male should have brought at least that. Reid wasn't an ordinary wolf.

"You-you-you shouldn't be here. Eze-Eze-Ezekiel should be the Itan and I just have to kill you and then he'll come back." Gary moved his thumb as if to cock the weapon again. Yeah, the male wasn't the smartest bear in the bunch, was he? "I-I-I missed at the doc's, I messed up and hurt the doc and Trisha, but I won't hurt anyone else now. J-j-just you."

"Right. So the drive-by didn't work and now you're here? Let me guess, you really expected the bullets to do the job, right? Or did you bank on the Carvrix?" He cataloged each expression that slid over Gary's face. Surprise and then fear. No, more than fear. Terror.

"How... He said..."

"Who's he, Gary?" The male's arm trembled, the barrel unsteady. "Ezekiel?" Gary nodded though Reid doubted he did it on purpose. The panic making him answer before he realized what he did. "Where'd he get it?"

"I-I-I..."

"Gary," Evie whispered, but Reid couldn't spare her a look. He'd already been shot six times—by this male, apparently—and he really didn't want to add another six to his count. Assuming Gary could shoot straight.

And if he didn't, and if he hit Evie, and if Evie died...

He'd kill the world.

Gary looked beyond him, the male's eyes landing on Reid's mate, and he decided he wasn't gonna wait for Gary to make his move. The male was going down. Now.

Without hesitation, he jolted forward, traveling the feet that separated them in an instant. Dirt flew as he ran, racing forward. His claws immediately formed, tips sharpening as his wolf shoved forward and demanded the bear's blood. He didn't care about Gary's threat to him. It was normal, anticipated even. He'd wondered who the first to betray the clan would be. Now he had his answer. Which meant he'd face off against Ezekiel sooner rather than later.

A cocky puppeteer like Zeke wouldn't take another failure well. First the drive-by and now this? Yes, they'd see him soon.

For now, Reid would handle this male.

Once Gary was within reach, Reid struck. Realization finally dawned on the bear's face, the knowledge that he wasn't leaving the clearing alive gradually overtaking his features. That's when the gun tried to swing toward Reid.

Tried.

Because one of Reid's claw-tipped hands scraped Gary's ribs, nails sinking into flesh and then dragging toward his abdomen in one gutting swipe that had muscle and bone exposed to the air. The other snatched the gun, hand wrapping around the cylinder and the flesh between his thumb and pointer stopping the hammer from striking a bullet. He twisted, wrenching the revolver from Gary's hand in one swift move and then he tossed the weapon aside. A hunk of metal wouldn't solve his problem.

Only death by claw would. There was nothing more satisfying than ripping apart a threat to Reid's happiness. Piece by piece.

Loss of the weapon and the injury made Gary desperate, made the bear stare at Reid with wild, panicked eyes that quickly transformed to bear. And then the rest of his body tried to follow suit. The snap and crack of bones, the rapid appearance of fur, and the midnight nails that formed on his human fingers told him the male was on the edge of losing control. Hell, as seconds passed, Reid realized they'd passed the edge and dove into the deep end of "shit's about to get fucked."

Normally, he would have let them male gather his fur and fought him hand to claw, but he had Evie to think about. He didn't want to risk Gary getting his paws on Reid's mate.

So he stopped it. Not with words since that wouldn't have been nearly as much fun, but with a punch right to the bear's reshaping jaw. He followed that up with a quick jab to Gary's nose and then an uppercut to his chin. Gary stumbled back, balance thrown off by the rapid rain of punches, and Reid followed him, not giving an inch.

"Bears rely on their size." Knee. Slice. Punch. "Instead of training bodies." Punch. Cut. Kick. "For a rapid shift." Kick. Knee right into his nose. "Because that's when you're most vulnerable."

The body that'd been perverted by the half-shift was now broken and twisted with Reid's treatment. The face that'd eased toward bear was now nothing more than a mottled perversion of Gary's human visage. The midnight claws were gone, human nails back as the male's animal retreated. It knew it'd lost. Gary's human half just hadn't realized it yet. The leg that'd reshaped to a bear's snapped under Reid's next kick and the knee collapsed with the second. It left Gary kneeling on the ground, swaying and still swinging his arms as if Reid would allow himself to be injured.

"You think you're too big to fall." He grabbed Gary's head and yanked it down, forcing his knee to collide with the male's face. "When really, you're too big to stand on two feet. And when we're on the same level, we're even." He released Gary, letting him fall to the side in a broken heap.

Reid knelt next to the bloody body and met the male's eyes. "I'm going to kill you." He ignored Gary's whimper. "Not because you followed the wrong male. Ignorance isn't an excuse, but it's an explanation. I would have let you live if you had come to me. But you shot at me, didn't you? You tried to get me and almost killed two humans." The broken male's eyes widened and he shook his head. Well, as much as he could. "I heard you, Gary. It wasn't supposed to be this way. And by trying to kill me, you risked my mate. By coming here with a gun, you risked my mate. For that, you'll die."

Fear, then panic, then acceptance. They were known to him, the emotions that flashed across broken features just before Reid ended a life. Long ago, he would have been swayed by that initial wave of fear, possibly even the panic, but with time came his own acceptance of what had to be done.

He didn't enjoy the act of killing, but he reveled in the relief that came from eliminating a threat. A movement to his right stole his attention for a moment and he spied Evie standing nearby, hands clutching the revolver as if it'd protect her from the world.

That was his job.

And the first step was ridding the planet of Gary. He wanted to take his time and play with his prey—his wolf was all for that idea—but he wanted to hold Evie more than he wanted to draw out Gary's death. So he cupped Gary's cheeks and then changed his hold. Reid tightened his grip and then one wrench ended the male's life. One moment he breathed and the next he... didn't.

And Reid didn't feel an ounce of remorse.

Dammit, this was another death he'd have to tell Clary about. He was really getting tired of this shit. He hated talking to his therapist. Hated. It.

He dropped Gary to the ground and pushed to his feet, wiping his hands on his stained jeans as he stood. Staring down at the body, his first thought was about the waste of a life. Because of Ezekiel. Zeke was the cause, Reid was simply the instrument.

Betrayal meant death.

"Hey, Reid?" Evie drew his attention and he watched her pad closer, her face getting redder by the step.

He looked her over, eyes traveling over her curved body and hunting for any hint of injury, noting she still clutched the gun. He'd pushed her off him when Gary attacked, but maybe he was too rough with her. Had he injured her when—

"Reid?"

Reid yanked his attention from the juncture of her thighs, realizing that his quick check somehow turned into him aching to lap at her cream again. "Huh, yeah?"

"You wanna know what I think is sexy?"

He quirked an eyebrow. "Now you wanna talk about sexy? Now?"

"Well, yeah." She grinned and nibbled her lip, attention flicking down and then she met his gaze once more. "I think it's hot as hell that you kicked Gary's ass with your dick hanging out."

Reid sighed and looked down his body, spying the aforementioned dick. "Well, shit."

Chapter Seventeen

Evelyn tried not to lean against him. Tried not to slump into his hard, warm body and take comfort in his embrace.

She was too pissed. At Reid, at Asher, at any damn person who thought the bonfire was a good idea.

"So, to recap, you expect Ezekiel to make an appearance and we're going to go through with the celebration anyway." She wasn't talking to any one person, but to the group of idiots all together.

"Yes?" She would have thought Asher's timid response and little-boy-lost smile was cute if they weren't talking about violence and death.

"This just can't happen. How do any of you think this is a good idea?" She met each male's gaze. She'd finally been introduced to them all, a dozen men who'd come at the Southeast Itan's request. A couple—she'd learned—were staying on once all was said and done. They liked Reid—to a point—and knew he'd be a good leader even if he did howl instead of roar. But no matter what, they knew he was a good leader, strong and fiercely protective of everything he called his.

Which was good. Until he decided to do stupid things such as bait her uncle.

Her attention drifted from Asher to Carter and then on to Mac, Ethan, and Blake. Those were the five who'd decided to stick around so she'd made it a point to remember them.

The other idiots—because they were all idiots since they supported this plan—weren't as important to her. Her bear didn't want them to get hurt, but the she-bitch had decided the males sticking around were hers and she needed to know everything about them. They'd live in the clan den with her and Reid, supporting their Itan twenty-four seven.

The others were good bears, but these males had become essential to keeping her mate alive.

Alive while he made himself vulnerable to Zeke.

"Seriously? No one has a response to this?"

"Evie…" Asher started and before she could correct him, Reid snarled at the male.

"Itana," her mate snapped and she sighed.

"Evelyn, Asher."

"No," her mate grumbled. "I'm the Itan, you're the Itana. Period."

"We haven't mated." She had to point out the obvious.

"Not for lack of desire. Zeke kicked your ass. I got shot. Then Zeke tried to get us shot, and I won't feel comfortable mating you until we're safe and I kill him."

That was sweet in a very bloody way. "Reid…"

He gave her a gentle squeeze, warm hands tightening on her thigh, and she turned her head to meet his stare. "This isn't a good plan."

"It's a perfect plan. He'll be there. He won't want to see his brothers burned. It's an insult and he won't let it stand."

It was an insult and he wouldn't let it stand. Burning basically said—to shifters—the three men never existed. Their ashes would be taken by the wind as if they'd never walked the land. Being buried was a sign of respect, of giving back to the Earth that supported you during life.

Ashes were nothing.

"How are you going to accomplish this? You're still injured—"

"It's hardly a twinge," he immediately countered.

The bullet wounds were a soft blush pink now, the redness gone as his wolf purged itself of the poison that stunted healing.

"—and he's not dumb enough to think you wandered off on your own to be taken out."

"Agreed."

She raised her eyebrows, waiting for him to finish and got… nothing.

"And…" she led, hoping he'd finish.

"And I won't be alone."

"Who'll be with you?"

His warm, callused hand cupped her cheek and she leaned into his palm, taking comfort in his touch. They weren't mated so the connection didn't soothe her bear as much as it would if they were tied together, but they'd come closer in the last few days. "Do you trust me?"

"Of course, I trust you." Not that she had a million reasons why exactly, but her bear told her she was never safer than at Reid's side. Period. "But that doesn't change the ques…" Her mind followed the twists and turns until she got to the only answer. "I'll be with you."

The five men joining their clan grumbled and growled, obviously not liking the plan. Well, Evelyn was slowly coming around to Reid's way of thinking.

"You'll be with me. We'll run off, pretend to find a nice spot to mate." Reid nuzzled her neck, licking the length of her throat. "I'll strip you bare."

"Oh," she whispered and tilted her head to the side, giving him more space.

"And when he thinks you're vulnerable, he'll strike." He sucked on her flesh and she squirmed, enjoying his sensual attentions way too much with this many people staring at them. "And then I'll kill him."

Thoughts of blood should have washed away her arousal.

It didn't.

Which made her realize she was slowly becoming more like Reid ever minute. And that… wasn't a bad thing. At all. She liked his view, liked that violence was dealt with swiftly and permanently. That he was so dedicated to the clan and his people, he would kill for them. There were fierce Itans across the country, men who ruled by intimidation and threats. Reid ruled by hard truths. If you hurt him or his, you were hurt in return, two fold.

A person only hurt one of his once because then… they were dead.

He'd proved that already, hadn't he?

And she… loved him for it. Or as close to love as she could feel after so short a time. No matter what it was called, he'd become necessary to her just as she was necessary to him.

"And me?"

"The second he's distracted, you climb. I don't want you close when he loses it. He'll get desperate and I want you out of the way."

"I could help," she pointed out. "I could shift and—"

Reid's denial was immediate. "I'm sure your bear is very strong, my wolf wouldn't want to claim a weak female, but you've never trained your shifts to be fast."

"I'm quick," she glared at him. "The quickest of my last clan."

"Two heartbeats, Evie. That's what it takes for me and when I push, I can get it down to one though not with any regularity. So while he's trying to pull on his fur, I will be there. If he shows up as a bear, it takes a single thought to bring my own forward. He will not win. It is just a matter of how long it'll take for him to die."

Damn he was sexy.

"Reid—"

He cut her off with a kiss, a quick brush of passion against her mouth that had her sinking fully into him and taking what he offered. It was hope and a promise, assurances that the night wouldn't end with him dead or dying, but with him killing his opponent. There was no other option for him. No other acceptable outcome.

And that was what he gave her. Right that moment, right then and there.

I will not be harmed.

I will not be killed.

I will end his life.

And he would. She knew he would. She just hated that it put her mate at risk.

"I will be fine," he murmured against her mouth.

"I know," she whispered back. And she did.

"So we'll go ahead with our plans."

Evelyn nodded. "We'll go ahead with our plans."

Even if she hated them.

"Good," his gaze left hers to focus on the gathered men and she did the same. "I want you all stationed around the edges of the clearing, monitoring the perimeter. Our bears are only allowed to head north for their run. Tell them their Itan ordered it since he cleared the area and ensured it was safe. Lie about booby traps or bombs if you have to, but they go north."

"And you two?" Asher was the only one ballsy enough to speak up.

"We go south. No one on our tails. He'll scent you."

A low snort had them all focusing on the door to the office and Mac swung it open before the eavesdropper could scamper away.

Scamper. Because that's what twelve-year-old girls did.

"Have something to say, Simone?" her mate drawled and her half-sister squirmed in place, fingers squeezed together.

"Um…"

"Spit it out before I send your butt back upstairs," Reid growled and she shot a glare at her mate. She was a kid, Simone…

"You're an idiot if you think he'll scent you," Simone's voice whipped through the silence and Evelyn realized that Reid might be damn justified with his anger.

But instead of yelling, her mate smiled widely. Which was… weird. "Ballsy, kid." Then his smile disappeared. "Explain."

Her sister stepped into the room, taking hesitant strides past the gathered men. "I told you they don't know how to track. Or scent. They learned when they were younger, but then granddaddy and," Simone met Evelyn's stare. "Granddaddy and your mom were killed by the four of them. Dad beat on your mom even though they were true mates and Granddaddy tried to stop them and…" Simone shrugged.

And that was that and exactly what she'd suspected. Not the beatings, not her mom's abuse, but she imagined that was how things had progressed. The four Archers were too mean to do anything but kill what stood in their way.

"They knew how to take care of themselves in the wild once, but never bothered to do it anymore. They can buy a whole cow from the butcher. Why hunt a deer?"

It was Evelyn's turn to snort. "There's nothing better than fresh."

Agreements were murmured around the room, the other shifters appreciating a new kill as much as she did.

"Okay," Reid nodded. "Then we'll use that." Reid's expression turned earnest. "Thank you, Simone. You're still going back upstairs, though. I'll hold a true clan gathering in a few days and you can come to that one."

"But you said you'd take out Zeke. Why can't—"

Reid moved fast, hand darting out and snatching Simone, yanking her close and her sister squeaked. Evelyn tensed but she wasn't worried about her mate, but more about how Simone would react. "Because if shit goes to hell, I refuse to risk you. You're Evie's sister which makes you mine and I sure as hell wouldn't allow Zoey into danger like this. I need Evie as part of the bait. Otherwise her happy ass would be home with you where women belong."

Evelyn glared at him.

"Duuude," Asher groaned. "I don't have a mate and I know that was a bad idea. Apologize. Otherwise you're gonna have one cold mating bed."

Reid glared at Asher. "Why?"

Now Asher shook his head. "First rule of mating—never ask why you need to apologize, just do it. A glare requires an apology. Aaaand now you've ruined it because you bothered to ask." The bear sighed. "You really should call Ty in Grayslake. Or his Enforcer, Van. Even Keen. Or Isaac. They're mated, they'll tell you."

Reid growled, the sound rolling through her, the vibrations plucking her nerves and arousal slid into her veins. She was mad at him, she had to remember that. But then he made those sounds…

"I don't need anyone to tell me how to handle my mate."

And then her desire fell flat. "Reid?"

"What?" he snapped.

"One, don't snap at me. Two, he's right. I'll explain why, later. For now, we need to get ready to go."

With that, she slipped from his lap and strode toward the door, ignoring the smack of skin on skin and the snarl that answered the action. She imagined Asher whacking Reid for screwing up and she… liked it. She liked that her mate was being called to the carpet as well as the knowledge that he was close enough to someone else to allow them that liberty without retaliation. He may have gone after Owen, but there was more than a passing acquaintance between Reid and Asher.

She'd make Asher cookies later.

Chapter Eighteen

Reid was gonna kill Asher later. Bloody. Painful. Long and drawn out. He'd torture the male for days.

Not because Ash had been right, but because the male hadn't told him to shut up before he'd pissed Evie off.

Now he tromped through the woods after Evie toward the gathering, trying not to stare at her ass as he followed her. He'd made that mistake once already, stared at her butt and imagined nibbling the plump globes, only to be caught. That had her glaring at him and when he looked to his Enforcer for help, Ash glared at him too.

He was not made for this mating shit. Give him an easy lay any day.

Okay, that was a lie. His dick—and wolf—didn't want anyone but Evie Archer even if she hated him a little bit at the moment.

When she looked over her shoulder and flashed him another glare, he knew enough was enough. She needed to get over being pissed already.

Using speed he'd learned long ago, Reid darted forward and snatched her, spinning them until she was pressed against a tree, their bodies aligned chest to chest.

She squeaked and pushed against him, but he ignored her, leaning down to bury his face in her hair. He licked the juncture of her shoulder and neck, aching to sink his teeth into that bit of flesh. She moaned with the action and tilted her head to the side to give him more room.

"I need you to not be angry with me anymore, Evie. I can't go into this clan gathering with you furious."

"Reid," she sighed and relaxed against him.

It was submission through sex and he wished it was because she trusted him—trusted in him. But he'd take what he could get. "You know what I've lost, Evie. I keep saying this, it is probably gonna drive you crazy by the time we're old and gray with a dozen kids and two dozen grandkids, but I can't let anything happen to you."

He didn't care if he sounded like a pussy. It was the truth.

Evie's breath caught, her heartbeat picking up a rapid pace. "Dozen?"

He smiled against her damp skin. "At least." He pulled back and met her gaze, his stare steady. "I want a life with you. Ezekiel's standing in the way. I also want you safe and as far away from him as possible. If I had my choice, you'd be behind a locked door, but I need you for this. So, quit giving me shit, lemme make you safe, and then you can yell at me later. I need to have my head on right for this. I can't do that if you're pissed at me."

Bare bones truth and it made him seem like a little bitch, but there was no denying his feelings.

"Okay," she whispered.

"Okay?" He pulled back, eyebrows raised. "Really?"

"Yeah, really. I wasn't... I haven't..." She licked her lips, the plump flesh glistening and reminding him of what they'd looked like wrapped around his dick. "I never thought past today. I mean, I never want to lose you but I didn't really consider life after all this. I just... kids. Grandkids. Life. I want that." A single tear slid down her cheek and he cursed himself for making her cry.

"Aw, baby, don't cry on me now."

"No," she shook her head. "They're good tears. I just realized that you... You're thinking of the future. You're planning ahead and I'm in it with you."

"You're my mate. Of course you are." His mate was damn beautiful but maybe she'd been dropped on her head as a child.

"Yeah, I just hadn't really thought about it. I was focusing on the choices you're taking away in the short term but you're taking those choices away because of what you want in the future. You're not being controlling so much as you're trying to protect what we'll have."

The way she smiled at him, the dreamy look in her eyes, was a hell of a lot better than her anger. So, if that was what she wanted to believe, he'd let her. Especially since the more he thought about her words, the more he realized she might be right.

But he wasn't a sentimental dick no matter what she said.

"That mean you're gonna stop giving me shit?"

Evie rolled her eyes. "Yes, it means I'm gonna stop giving you shit."

He didn't have anything to say to that, so he just grunted and pulled back, yanking her along with him as he returned to their trek through the forest. It took longer to reach the clearing than it had earlier in the day, but he wasn't chasing his mate through the trees this time, either. They took their time, scenting the air and keeping their eyes open as they sought Ezekiel. He didn't imagine the male would show up so early, just as the sun disappeared, but a male could hope.

They finally stepped free of the forest and he paused to let his gaze sweep the glen. His bears—his—filled the empty space, groupings of men and women scattered around the clearing, waiting for him to start the gathering. The females most affected by the Archers were off to one side, huddled together and clinging to one another. He'd never done anything to make them wary, but he didn't really have to. He scared others by existing. Hopefully they'd get used to him, let him in so he could help them heal.

Seeing them, he glanced back at the males trailing after them.

"Owen," he kept his voice low so he wouldn't draw attention. Or rather, more attention.

The younger man bolted forward. "Itan?"

"Is there anything that should be addressed? Did anyone come forward and request help? Have something to report?"

Owen's gaze drifted to the small group of females. "Nothing to report. They are... injured," he paused. "But I think you've handled the problems already." Owen stepped closer, dropping his voice lower. "They have a lot of healing, Itan. They've been," he paused once more. "Forced. Repeatedly. Two had their mates killed in front of them. They... it was bad. And you've helped with a lot of it by taking out the Archers, but they're always gonna be afraid of you. Of what you can do and represent."

He wasn't surprised. Saddened but not surprised.

Reid nodded. "Let me know if we can help."

At the we, Evie squeezed his hand as if thanking him for including her. What the hell? Of course he included her. He couldn't do anything without her.

"Yes, Itan." And like that, Owen retreated, easing to the back of their group, but his gaze remained trained on the cluster. His expression was one of heartache and... need?

Aw, shit. If Owen wanted one of the women, he knew he'd never be rid of the male. That sucked.

Pushing the annoyance to the back of his mind, he strode forward, Evie at his side, until they reached the center. All conversation ceased entirely as he took his spot. The group slowly circled around him until they each took a seat on the grass.

"I'm Reid Bennett, your new Itan."

"You're a wolf," a male shouted from the back and Reid held onto his control by a thread.

"Thank you, Captain Obvious. Yes, I'm a wolf. Yes, I killed your Itan. Yes, I killed his brothers. And yes, I will kill the last who still evades me." He paused, attention drifting over the bears before him. "I was going to come up here and explain my past. I was going to tell you I ended a wolf pack for harming my sister. That I destroyed half of a hyena pack because of what they did to my mother. I was going to explain how I came to be here and lay out why I will make your clan a good Itan."

Another pause, one giving them a chance to absorb his words. "But the truth is, any other male who stood before you, the last Itan's blood on his claws, wouldn't have to answer a single question. This means I will not, either. You can choose to stay and follow a wolf who claims this position by death or you can leave. You are welcome to request assistance from the Southeast Itan. In fact, you can use my cell phone to make the call." He dug into his jeans, and tossed the device toward the group.

"Speed dial one will get Terrence. He knows me, he sent me, and he'll help you get away from me if that is your choice. If I find out you were part of the madness that overtook this clan, I will force you out myself. And no phone call will save you then." Seconds ticked past, no one moving. Some would. Maybe not while they were all gathered together, but he didn't doubt that some would leave.

"If you stay, I will remain dedicated to you. No one will hurt you and if they dare, the pain you experience will be avenged on the idiot who was dumb enough to touch what belongs to me. You are mine. You will be mine. I am not crazy. I am possessive. I do not glory in blood, but in retribution. I do not enjoy violence, but welcome it with open arms when it comes to someone who harmed someone I claim.

"If that means I strike out at one of our own members, then that's what it means. No crime will remain unpunished, no matter the offender. You will be safe from me and from yourselves."

He let the quiet envelope them, let it drift over them, and he drew in the scents that flowed from the bears. There was anger and fear. Happiness and concern. Emotions he expected. Emotions he welcomed.

Then there was another. A twisted, sticky, burning hate that crept into his pores.

Ezekiel.

He'd come, the stupid bastard.

Good for Reid. Not so good for Zeke.

"Think about what I've said. Consider your options and make your own choices without threat of retribution. For now, I'm going to run with my mate," he held up their joined hands, showing off the fact that he and Evie stood together. "And I'm going to claim her. So, to preserve a little of her modesty, I ask that you hunt north. Evie and I will head south."

"What about the…" A timid female voice drew his attention and she slowly rose to her feet. "What about our…" She trembled and cupped her stomach protectively.

Evie gave his hand a gentle squeeze so he let her handle this one, allowing her to pull her hand free before she padded toward the shaking bear. Soon the woman was in his mate's arms, soft shushes reaching his ears until she no longer shook and then it was his mate who turned and spoke to the gathered bears. "If you have children from or are pregnant with children fathered by my uncles or Patrick, they are welcome here. No one is going to throw you out. You belong to us. All of you. Two feet, four feet, or still in the womb, you are ours."

Some of the fear bled away with his mate's words and he knew he could not have picked a better—stronger—female had he tried. Evie was perfect. Deliciously, lusciously, perfect.

She turned to him, their gazes clashing and he hoped she saw the emotions that filled him. Possessiveness, sure. But there was happiness. Desire. Need. Something he might think of as love, but he wasn't sure what that emotion felt like. It was what he felt for his sister, but more. So much, much more. Indescribable yet so basic. It encompassed everything inside him and yet left a part of him empty.

The part that was supposed to come from her. The other half of his soul.

It was love then. That's what others called their mates. Soul mates.

That's what they had.

And he was about to put it at risk.

Evie whispered to the woman and then passed her off to another obviously pregnant female. His gut churned, his ache to destroy Ezekiel growing by the moment. He'd already destroyed the others, but at least he had one left to massacre.

He couldn't wait.

Soon Evie was at his side once more, her fingers twined with his, and he knew it was time. He turned his head and spoke to Asher. "Do it." His Enforcer immediately spoke into his phone, passing on Reid's message, and he spoke once more. "Look to the west." Not a single person denied him, each bear turning to stare behind them and then a fireball of red and yellow exploded into the sky, the fire burning high and bright. "That is your past. It's gone. Destroyed as if it never existed. And I," dozens of eyes were now trained on him. "I am your future."

Evie elbowed him. "We," she hissed and it was exactly what the crowd needed. A handful of chuckles passed through the crowd, smiles accompanying the sounds.

"We are your future."

Chapter Nineteen

Hell yeah, they were the clan's future.

I am your future.

Evelyn would give him a future. Six feet in the ground, that was going to be his future.

I am your future.

Ha!

Evelyn stomped through the foliage, Reid on her tail, but thankfully silent. Self-preservation, probably.

I am your future.

Ooh…

Argh.

"Evie," he called after her, but she didn't stop.

"Evie." Nope, still not stopping.

"Dammit, Evie." Oh, sure, that'd get her to stop.

Next, he growled. That was it, a single growl. Followed by a low oomph—from her—as he tackled her. Tackled her, but cradled her as well.

"Evie," he sighed and she had to admit their new position was nice.

He'd rolled them so she landed on top, much like the fun they'd had earlier in the day. When Gary came after Reid with a gun.

She crawled from atop him, worried that somehow Zeke would get the drop on them and then her uncle would hurt her mate and then...

He didn't let her go, instead, wrapping his arms and legs around her so she couldn't move. "Hey, calm down," he murmured. "Stay with me." He cradled her skull and urged her to lower her head. "Don't leave me."

She was going to stay alert. She was. Really. But then he licked her neck and nibbled her ear and his cock grew hard and, and, and...

And she sighed once more, relaxing into him and letting him do as he desired. So when he changed their positions, moving until she was on her back beneath him and he hovered above her, she didn't protest. Not when his hands teased her skin, plucked at her buttons until her shirt parted to slowly expose her pale flesh.

"Have I told you how beautiful you are?"

"Once or twice," she gave him a soft smile. "But a girl likes to hear that she's appreciated."

"Baby, you're gorgeous and I'm so damned lucky I get to keep you." He cupped her breast, thumb flicking over her hardening nipple. "Forever."

This was for show and yet it wasn't. They were playing a part, but her body didn't get the memo because when he pinched her nipple, she moaned. And when he tugged on it, she groaned. And when he snapped her bra strap and lowered the bra cup to expose her... she gasped and then moaned and groaned.

She was supposed to focus on their surroundings. But how when all she could think about was his cock in her pussy, threats be damned.

Reid knew exactly what he was doing. That cocky smirk and his sparkling eyes told her that he was fully aware of her reactions.

And he liked it.

Okay, she liked it too, but she didn't want to!

"Reid," she gasped and arched her back, pressing her breast against his palm. "Please."

"Please what?" His eyes flared brighter.

"Fuck me. Claim me." He'd only plucked her nipple, but she was so ready for him. Her pussy was slick and wet, memories of his mouth on her heat spurring her arousal.

Then his look changed, the desire and joy still present, but something else filled his expression. A wariness, a readiness that she'd witnessed before they'd entered the clearing. As if his body was prepared for whatever came at him.

The wolf lurked beneath the surface of Reid's skin even if Evelyn couldn't see clear evidence of its presence. His muscles were tense—not with need, but restrained violence. His nostrils flared and his amber eyes brightened, the wolf in her mate catching a scent that excited him.

She waded through the desire and cravings for him and sought out what Reid discovered. And found... Zeke.

Close.

She'd almost forgotten their purpose, overcome by pleasure when their true purpose was capturing and killing her uncle.

That was something she'd adopted from Reid, a distance between what her human mind perceived as right and wrong and that of her bear. The bear didn't have a problem with what was about to happen while her human half felt a twinge of regret.

The bear told her to man up.

And instead of arguing with the animal, she gave in. I'm trying.

Reid continued his attentions and she continued to spur him on, giving him the drawn out whimpers and moans he expected, but they saw the truth in each other's eyes. Zeke was close... watching... waiting.

How far would their party go before he struck?

"Let's take this off, baby," Reid murmured, tugging at her other bra strap. It took two slices total. One for the left strap and another at the center so he could brush the rest of the fabric away. Now she was bared to him, breasts growing heavy and aching for his touch. "You're so gorgeous." He cupped her tits, tormenting her nipples once more. "I don't know where to put my mouth first."

"Well, I have my own ideas." She wiggled her eyebrows and Reid released a short laugh.

"Pain in the ass."

Evelyn grinned. "Not yet."

"Evie—"

That was it. The last word before her world erupted in a mass of brown fur and angry snarls. In a whirlwind of claws and fangs and...

* * *

Reid was ready for the strike and when it came, he rolled with the movement. So when the bear meant to pounce and drive him to the ground, Reid ensured the male overshot his mark and stumbled across the leaf-littered ground. He didn't spare a look for Evie, knowing she'd do as he said. They'd talked about this and he had to believe she'd listen at least now. Who knew what the future would hold.

In bear form, Zeke scrambled for purchase, claws digging into dirt and foliage as he fought to right himself. And he let the male find his feet, looking forward to an almost fair fight.

Almost because there really was no way for a fight to be fair if Reid was one of the opponents. Zeke was a dead bear breathing.

Ezekiel roared, mouth wide and spit dripping from his fangs and spraying from his mouth with the movement.

"Impressive." Reid agreed. It was loud if not threatening. "Come peacefully, and I'll end you quickly."

He always had to give a choice, give someone a chance to save themselves some agony. Some called him soft.

They only ever said it once.

Unfortunately for Zeke, he wouldn't give in.

Fortunately for Reid... Zeke wouldn't give in.

"Your party, then." Reid grinned and waited, meeting Zeke's gaze, the bear staring at him as it calculated its next move.

Most were afraid of a predator larger than themselves. Reid always thought of them as a challenge.

How big of an animal can I kill?

So far, it was a feral polar bear.

Ezekiel lumbered forward, mouth gaping and neck extended at his rushed approach. It was something Reid saw from a mile away, the male's attempt at surprise ending with a punch to the bear's jaw. It wasn't enough to break it—and he was pretty sure he cut his knuckles on a couple teeth—but it stunned the male. Stunned it enough for Reid to bring his claws forward to scrape the other side of Zeke's face. Punch on the right, gouges on the left and that put Ezekiel's left out of commission.

In fact, Reid shook his left paw, did he have an eyeball stuck to a claw? Ew. Yes, yes he did. Gross. Blood was one things, but eyeballs always creeped him out.

But he didn't have much time to consider the eyeball when Zeke swung at him, his own paw splayed wide and claws extended as he reached for Reid. He easily ducked the strike while he scraped his nails down the bear's side. Blood coated his paw, the warm, coppery fluid flowing over his gray fur, staining it red.

Zeke danced away, shying from Reid's attack, but it wasn't quick enough. Not when Zeke tried the exact same thing and Reid repeated the motion on the animal's other side.

"There, a matching set." He grinned at the bear, malice and joy warring within him.

Zeke wanted to give him his own set, the bear giving it a shot once more. Trading him blows, but never landing a single one. Strike, dodge, cut. Over and over again. He worked to tire out the massive male, giving Zeke exactly what he'd promised.

"You could have avoided all this pain if you just would have—"

Nothing. Would have done nothing because Reid was a cocky asshole who didn't pay attention to where he stepped and tripped on a root. On a motherfucking root.

At least his dick wasn't hanging out. That was a bonus.

Zeke flashed his fangs, the excitement unmistakable in the bear's eyes. He ran at Reid, pouncing while Reid tried to regain his feet. The massive paws bracketed him, caging him like an animal, while those massive teeth descended. Zeke's jaws were spread widely, saliva dripping onto Reid and those fangs glistened in the darkness.

Destructive. Dangerous. Deadly.

Reid wrapped his hands around Zeke's throat, grasping and holding the male, not allowing him to crush Reid's skull with a single bite. He had a future to plan. He wasn't about to die now. He just had to figure out how to get out of the bullshit mess he'd created. Zeke snapped and snarled, jolting and jerking against Reid's hold, but he held fast, refusing to allow the bear freedom.

A feminine shout—Evie—reached him, but he didn't allow his attention to be diverted. Not when life and death lingered so close.

Ezekiel put his body weight into the push, battling to close his deadly jaws over Reid's head. Not happening. Not when he had so much to live for. So he transformed his claws further. He let the wolf slink past his control and truly join the fight. He dug his nails into Zeke's vulnerable throat, talons sinking deep and slicing into flesh and muscle. He'd make Zeke bleed to death before he let the bear take him.

They stared at one another, bear and wolf, gazes colliding and the wolf roared at the size of the bear's balls. He dared to stare Reid down? He dared?

The bear would die for that alone, fuck all of his other transgressions.

Fingers digging deeper also lessened the distance between their faces, the flesh parting and allowing him to press down even further. And... this was the time he kinda hoped Zeke would bleed to death.

But Ezekiel snapped his jaws, jerking forward with each bite, trying to grasp at some of Reid's flesh. Each move brought them closer. Each move pushed them nearer to an end to their struggles. Those deadly fangs were now no more than an inch from Reid, taunting him with the end, and he fought what was to come.

He'd been a cocky asshole and now he'd suffer the consequences.

He'd assured the clan they were safe.

He'd assured his bears he would be fine.

He'd assured Evie this battle would be fierce, but fast. They would mate soon.

He'd... never anticipated losing.

Cocky. More than that. He'd begun to care. He never cared for anyone before. He'd never worried over anyone. He was a body going through the motions, a frame filled with the need for violence and vengeance. Having Evie, having Brookfield, changed him. For the better, sure.

But also worse since he was fairly sure he was about to meet his maker. Or tormentor. Heaven or hell, he'd hate them both because it meant he wouldn't have Evie.

"Reid!" Her shout came from far away. Distant and fearful and he wanted to reassure her, but he couldn't because—

The sound was familiar, a pop that was easily identifiable, but out of place in the middle of a battle between shifters. What made it odder was that the moment the sound struck his ears, something else struck... Zeke.

Brain matter scattered, blood and the spongy organ decorating the ground and Reid, coating him even further. But there was one unmistakable fact that could not be avoided.

Zeke was missing half his head.

Huh.

He looked around for Evie, annoyed yet proud of her for saving his ass. But it wasn't Evie who held the gun in trembling hands. It wasn't Evie who had tears overflowing her eyes. And it wasn't Evie who fell to the ground, hands cupping her rounded belly, weapon forgotten on the forest floor.

"Katherine," his mate whispered and then rushed to the crumpled female. "Oh, Katherine."

"He-he-he…" Katherine sobbed. "I needed to do it. I had to. I had to. I had…"

Evie pulled the pregnant woman into her arms and he met his mate's gaze over Katherine's head. What he saw there, a mirror of Katherine's heartbreak and pain, stole any hint of anger at the bear's interference.

Yes, Reid needed Ezekiel gone, but Katherine… needed vengeance.

Chapter Twenty

Reid wasn't sure how to feel. Wasn't sure how to live with the new knowledge and realizations that plagued him. He had half a mind to call Clary and talk this shit out, but he didn't want her in Brookfield any quicker than necessary.

So he was stuck thinking it over himself, wondering how he could hold onto a clan when he nearly had his ass handed to him by Zeke and had to be saved by Katherine. Did he deserve to be the Itan? Did he deserve to call himself a bear, period?

Fuck if he knew though he wished he did.

For now, he had to figure out how to deal with last night's drama and heal the clan today. At least he could walk without an escort. With Zeke's death came other knowledge, other realizations. The clan still held a few who enjoyed a higher status due to the Archers. Those who had participated when the Archer males dragged women kicking and screaming into the clan den. He didn't know who they were, but he'd find out.

Then there was the fact that Brookfield wasn't the only screwed up clan due to the Archer family. There were others who played with Brookfield men and women. Other Itans who came to town to play with clan members. Those that provided Carvrix to Ezekiel.

It was a twisted web that disgusted and angered him. Even if he didn't know every member of his clan, he was consumed with rage over what they'd endured. They'd culled the few Archer sympathizers he could identify, packaged them up and shipped them to Terrence. Reid didn't have time to deal with them. Not when he had a house filled with bears who needed his attention.

And they'd get it. After he took time to just breathe for a second. The walls had closed in on him, suffocating him with responsibility. He needed a place without walls, without tethers, without people.

He found it in the forest, boots tromping over now familiar ground as he delved deeper and deeper until… he came across a wide patch of dark brown. Some of the grass was painted red, but the dirt had absorbed a lot of the blood. Insects had carted off some of the chunks of flesh and brain. Whatever they'd left behind when they hauled the body to the massive fire they'd created for the other three Archers and Gary.

Evil purged from the earth.

Still left a stain though.

"Reid?" her voice was soft and hesitant. Almost timid. As if she was afraid of what he'd do with her intrusion.

Couldn't blame her. Last night had been… interesting. He'd lost it more than a little bit, the wolf furious at their kill being snatched from their paws. Today… today he was better. The animal didn't like Katherine's actions, but he couldn't begrudge her vengeance. Not when Evie drew the woman close, tight grip tugging the pregnant woman's top aside just enough to give Reid a glance at her scars.

Vengeance was hers. It'd been earned with every scarring cut and scrape and the child she carried.

"Hey, baby." He forced a grin to his lips and held out his hand for her, beckoning her forward. Whether he led the clan or not, he still had Evie. Unless she decided a wolf who'd lost a pack and possibly a clan was beneath her. That'd suck.

But he'd just kidnap her. She couldn't stay furious forever.

"You don't have to do that." She placed her hand in his and he slowly pulled her into his side.

"What?" He pressed a soft kiss to the top of her head.

"Pretend you're not angry. That you're not upset. That you're not unsettled."

He was all that and so much more. "I'm fine, Evie."

She shook her head. "No, you're not. And I know something—everything—is eating at you." She placed her hand over his heart and he covered hers with his own. "Tell me what's going on. How can I help you?"

"Evelyn," he sighed.

"Evie," she corrected him and he grinned. She liked the nickname as much as he did.

"Evie, it's nothing."

She shook her head again. "If it was nothing, you wouldn't be out here alone."

"It's fine."

"It's not."

Did she have to argue with him? "Baby…"

She ignored him and grasped his hand, yanking him behind her and he didn't have the strength to deny her. He followed like a docile lamb and if that wasn't out of character, he didn't know what was. He never followed. He led. He argued. He took control. He… Screw it. He let Evie take him wherever she wanted.

They skirted the clearing, traveling deeper into the forest, following her imaginary trail until he realized they were headed up a gradual slope. He didn't stop her, didn't nudge her or ask her where they were going. It was obvious his mate had a destination in mind and he allowed himself to enjoy their time together.

Minutes ticked past. An hour? Hour and a half? He wasn't sure. He just knew his wolf was aware of everything around them, conscious of their surroundings even as Reid's human side focused on Evie's ass.

He couldn't help it. It was a very nice ass. One he wanted to nibble and bite and…

A smaller clearing came into view, a break in the trees that opened to expose one of the most beautiful views he'd ever experienced. Sure, Grayslake was pretty. His hometown of Redby just as gorgeous. But this... Brookfield spread out before them in swaths of green. Rolling hills and the town settled snug in a basin. Pride and possessiveness surged inside him, his wolf telling him to man up and hold onto the town with both hands.

It was his.

His.

Just like Evie.

"Evie?"

She released him and padded to a large boulder that rested near the edge of the downward slope. She crawled atop the rock, drawing her knees up and wrapping her arms around her shins. She remained silent and he merely watched her, the way the wind picked up her hair and made it dance in the air, the way her head tilted when she met his gaze, and the line of her neck as she turned her attention back to the town below. "I came here expecting to hate it, you know. Every inch. Every second I was in town. But my grandmother willed it and I didn't have anyone else. It was what she wanted and the Itan told me I had to follow clan law. So I made plans and uprooted my life. Deciding I'd figure something out with medical school once I settled."

Reid edged closer, not stopping until he too leaned against the rock, arm around her shoulders. He couldn't not touch her. "And?"

"And I hated it when I got here. When I saw my father. When I saw what they did. It made me sick. It made me want to cry because their blood is in my veins."

"Then?"

"It made me angry. I couldn't stop them with my claws, but I could make a call. I could reach out."

"So you did."

"I did. And Terrence sent the answer to my prayers."

He shook his head and rested his cheek atop hers. "No, Evie, he didn't."

"Yes, no matter what you say, you are the perfect person for this town, for this clan."

"He nearly won."

"Nearly isn't actually."

And because she was his mate, his other half, he let his fears out. He wouldn't tell Clary, but Evie? He'd tell Evie. "It was close. What kind of Itan boasts about killing everything and then nearly dies? I'm a wolf. It'll take one determined bear…"

To take the clan from me. To take them all from me.

"It's a risk, Reid. Wolf or bear, things happen. Sometimes for the better, sometimes for the worse, but no matter what, you would have won if Katherine hadn't interfered."

"You give me more credit than I deserve."

Evie nuzzled him and he pulled her closer. "I give you what you've earned."

"I got cocky."

"True enough, but I think everything you've done warrants it."

"I'm weak."

"Never. I don't think you know how." Evie tilted her head back and he eased his attention from the town to her.

"I—"

"I think you're a different person now than when you met my father."

"I'm the same as I always was."

"No," her hand once again found its way to his chest. "You didn't have anything to fight for before Brookfield, before me. Now you do. It changed you. How you fight. How you think. How you feel. You're no less dangerous, Reid, you just might be a little more careful. You have something to live for now. Me. This town. This clan. Having feelings doesn't make you less."

"It almost got me killed." It was an agreement without agreement.

"Not knowing how to manage those emotions resulted in you struggling. You had so much rage—"

"It's always there."

"—but now it's tempered by love and you need to learn how to fight with that in your heart."

"Yeah." He couldn't refute her statement. There was no way to deny the truth.

"So instead of fighting without caring about whether you live or die, you learn how to fight while you make sure you live."

"You make it sound easy." He gave her a rueful grin.

"It is."

Reid moved until they faced one another, Evie still resting on the rock while he slowly eased her legs down until her thighs were spread. He stepped between them, making room for himself. "Loving you, Evie… that's easy."

"Then live for me. Stay for me. Fight for me. I'll go wherever you go, but you know this is home. You feel it."

He did.

He also felt something else. Felt his heart piecing itself back together, felt his ragged soul gradually gathering the tattered pieces of itself. And he realized it wasn't Clary that he needed in his life.

It was Evie.

Beautiful Evie. Gorgeous Evie. Unmated Evie.

"I'll do anything for you, Evelyn."

"Evie."

"Evelyn. Evelyn Bennett."

"We're not mated."

He grinned, heart feeling lighter by the second. "We can be in under five minutes."

She rolled her eyes, lips parting into a half smile. "At least I'm not mating a one minute man."

Chapter Twenty-one

Evelyn couldn't tear her eyes from Reid, from the intensity in his eyes or the cocky curve of his lips. He was hers. From head to toe. Hers.

"Definitely more than one minute." His gaze raked her from top to bottom, heat filling his expression and he licked his lips as if he couldn't wait to taste her. And she couldn't wait to be tasted, to feel his mouth on her skin and his fangs in her flesh. "Is this what you want?" He reached for her legs, teasing her outer thighs from knee and the farther north. "You want me to claim you? Make you mine?"

Her pussy heated, warming more and more the closer he got to where she desired him most. "Yes."

She had no other answer. She could give no other answer.

"Here? Now?" His fingers teased the edge of her shorts, dipping beneath the frayed hem and tickling her skin.

"Yes." It made sense. This was a quiet, special place she'd discovered not long after arriving. She'd made it hers. Now they'd make it theirs. Their spot to get away from the stress of ruling the clan. Somewhere they could retreat and simply be. "Here. Now."

No hesitation. Why would she? She wanted to belong to Reid. The strongest male she'd ever met, wolf and all.

His digits reached higher, hand delving beneath her shorts and gripping her legs. "I want you too badly to be gentle, Evie. The wolf craves you." A growl filled his voice, Reid's inner-wolf reasserting the statement. "He wants to mount you, cover you... bite you."

A shudder worked through her body and her pussy clenched. The idea of being taken, truly claimed, sent a wave of arousal crashing through her. Need snaked along her nerves, nipples pebbling in anticipation of his mouth, pussy clenching and aching to be filled. She pulsed with desire, his nearness and words spurring her impending ecstasy.

He would take her. Claim her.

She couldn't wait.

The hint of doubt filling his features had to be addressed. She knew his words were meant to scare her, but they did anything but. "I want that, Reid. I want your wolf. I'm not mating a human. I'm mating a male. Show me your wolf. Show me what being yours will be like."

She taunted the wolf and based on the amber now filling his eyes, the animal was taking the bait. Those teasing fingers squeezed her thighs, his nails pricking her skin and sending a jolt of pain up her spine. It didn't take away from the pleasure of his touch, but added to it, making it more.

"Evie…" he rumbled.

"Show me, Reid." She leaned into him, bringing their faces close and then darted forward to nip his lower lip. "Show me."

The low rumble turned into a snarl and growl. He snatched his hands from her legs and gripped her hips. In one whip fast move, he had her facing the boulder and bent at the waist. She caught herself, placing her elbows on the hard stone.

He clawed at her shorts, sharpened nails scraping the fabric and fighting with the button and zipper until warm air bathed her skin. He'd been nearly gentle in his treatment of her shorts, not fully destroying them, but her panties were a different story. Those were shredded with a few claws and one yank.

And she wasn't scared by his need, by his rough treatment. It was a testament to his desire and she reveled in his responses.

She yanked at her shirt and bra, tossing them aside so they wouldn't suffer the same fate as her panties.

"Beautiful," he rasped and she glanced over her shoulder, watching the changes in his expression when she shook her ass. Reid licked his lips, tongue darting out to wet them. His look turned hungry, desperate for a taste of her.

"Reid?"

"Mine," he snarled.

"Always yours." Her pussy clenched, reacting to his declaration. "Always."

He grunted and his hands returned to her shorts, pulling them farther down her legs. He tugged on one shoe, pulling it off and then helping her step out of her clothing enough so she wasn't hindered. Then he nudged her thighs apart even more until she was fully bared to his gaze.

"All mine."

"Make me yours." She taunted him, his wolf, and was prepared for the consequences. The wonderful, mind blowing consequences.

His cock was hard beneath his jeans, the bulge straining against the denim, and he palmed his dick through the fabric. He squeezed it hard, making the outline even starker. She couldn't help but remember his taste, the feel of him against her tongue. She wanted that again, wanted him filling her mouth as she cradled him and gave him pleasure.

She let her attention drift, rising higher until their eyes collided.

"Next time," he murmured. She wasn't sure what he was talking about. Not until he dropped to his knees behind her and his talented tongue lapped at her slit.

Next time she could taste him. For now, she was along for the ride.

He licked her, from clit to center he tormented her. He slipped up, circling her opening, before sliding back down to tap her clit.

"S'good," he rumbled against her flesh. "Fucking good."

Evelyn dropped her head forward, relaxing and focusing on the sensations Reid gifted her. Concentrated on the sweep of his tongue and the way he tormented her clit. On the random pattern and the way it spurred her pleasure. Her pussy clenched, tightening and milking, silently begging to be filled.

By Reid. By her mate.

But not yet. Not when he sucked on that bundle of nerves. Not when he scraped his tooth gently over that small nubbin.

Her legs shook with the bliss he caused, the feel of all that ecstasy racing over her nerves nearly making her fall with the overwhelming feelings. But she remained still, locking her knees and thanking nature for putting the boulder in this exact spot.

He licked her. Again and again, his growls slowly coming to mingle and dance with her moans and pleas. The sensations were dizzying, stealing her focus until she thought of nothing but Reid between her thighs.

Reid making her sigh.

Reid making her moan.

Reid making her groan.

Reid making her beg.

"Please…"

He growled low, the vibrations making her gasp and then sob, shoving and pushing her toward the edge of release. It was there, almost in her grasp, and Reid continued urging her on with every nip, lick, and suck.

Her legs trembled, body shaking as she was overcome with need. With a burning pleasure that threatened to overtake her in a frenzied explosion.

His hands gripped her hips, pulling her backward and harder against his mouth, his actions rough and seeming as desperate as she felt.

"Reid," she whimpered. "So close."

His next sound was a growl, low and deep, threatening and pleading at once. He wanted her to come and dammit, she wanted that too.

Then he captured her clit between his teeth.

Then he sucked.

Then he flicked.

Then… "Reid!"

Her shout echoed through the clearing, voice going on and on as the pleasure of her orgasm rocked through her body. It filled every inch of her, stretching to her toes, consuming her muscles and bones and saturating her blood.

Overwhelming spasms joined the molten sensations or her orgasm, her passion cresting and snatching any hint of control. She welcomed the shattering release and drew the ecstasy forward and then…

Then it got so much better. Between one heartbeat and the next Reid was there, his cock poised at her entrance.

And in one, fluid thrust, he filled her until she was stretched tightly around his dick and it was better than she'd ever imagined.

* * *

It was better than Reid had ever imagined. Being inside her, possessing her, was more pleasurable than his wildest dream or strongest hope.

He imbedded himself until their hips met, his cock firmly within her pussy. She squeezed him like a warm, wet velvet glove, her walls rippling around him as her orgasm stretched on. He never wanted it to end, wanted it to always welcome him and the ecstasy he could give her.

He withdrew, ignoring her whimper, and then pushed into her once more, pounding her as her release continued. He fought to meet her tempo, to work his hips in time with her unending moans and whimpering groans. Reid eased out and thrust forward, burying himself deep once more.

Slow and gentle or hard and relentless?

The harder he thrust, the tighter she squeezed him, and the more pleasure he drew from her.

Evie made the decision for him. So he picked up his pace, squeezing her hips as he adopted a punishing rhythm that had her calling out for him to give her more, to never stop, to make her come once more.

He was happy to grant her every wish.

He drove his cock into her over and over again, claiming her, absorbing her cries of pleasure. The harder he plunged, the louder she shouted, the more her yells spurred him toward the edge of release.

Her wetness rippled and milked him, seeming to silently plea for his cum. He wanted to pump her full, claim her from inside out until all would know she was his.

His.

Reid Bennett, abandoned wolf, clan Itan.

With each thrust, each meeting of their hips, her ass bounced and jiggled, taunting and teasing him. She was his. Every soft inch of her. This ass was his and he'd claim all of her someday. Once their world settled, he'd take her ass, own every part of her body.

For now, he teased her back entrance, thumb caressing the puckered opening and she clenched down on his dick even harder.

"Reid!" she sobbed but not in pain or pleading for him to stop. No, she wanted it. Wanted him.

"Mine," he snarled, his wolf needing to hear the words.

"Yours."

"Always mine." Always, always.

"Yes."

Their bodies came together in a lewd slap of skin on skin, the sounds of their lovemaking filling the clearing, the scent of their sex consuming the air. It was not just his flavors, but theirs.

Her pussy squeezed him tightly, convulsing around his shaft, and he fought his release. He wanted to keep pleasuring her and taking his own pleasure. But her heat wouldn't allow his lovemaking to continue.

She clenched even tighter, almost demanding he remain inside her, and he would. Soon. When he filled her with his cum and had his fangs buried in her shoulder.

His mouth watered, his pace remaining steady while he imagined the taste of her blood on his tongue. Hot and sweet, seductive and alluring.

He couldn't wait. Wouldn't wait.

"Evie," he rasped. "Need you to come on my cock." Needed it like air. "Give it to me."

"Reid, I can't..." she whined.

"You can." He would take nothing less. Keeping his pace steady, he reached around her, fingers unerringly finding her swollen clit. He circled and tapped the nub, her pussy squeezing him in response. "Do it. Come."

Then he assured the outcome, squeezing and pinching that bit of flesh gently before carefully scraping his thumbnail over the bundle of nerves.

It'd been what she needed, what she'd required to go flying over the edge. "Reid!"

Her bellow consumed him, sending his own pleasure spiraling until he could do nothing but follow her. His wolf rushed forward, fangs bared and ready to complete their mating while his human half embraced his release. It rushed through him in an unending wave of sensation that stole his control, wrenching it from his human grasp.

But the wolf... it still held a snippet of power. It shifted his teeth to wolfen fangs, pushing the canines free of his gums. And then it forced him into action. It had him leaning forward, mouth open and snarling a single word.

"Mine."

Evie looked over her shoulder at him, her eyes midnight with her bear's presence. "Yes."

The animal needed nothing else, no other assurances. He struck, sinking his fangs deep into her vulnerable flesh. His teeth pierced the skin with ease and blood filled his mouth. He swallowed convulsively and savored the flavors of the liquid. Sweet and tangy, salty with a hint of purity that was all that made up his mate.

His mate.

All his now.

He suckled and swallowed once more, spurring their orgasms to continue, sending them arching higher with each tug and pull. His balls emptied into her, his cock pulsing and twitching within her still rippling sheath.

His cock ached, overwhelmed by the pleasure turning to pain as he claimed his mate. He bathed her in his scent, showing one and all she was his.

By swallowing her blood, he was showing one and all he was hers.

A soft whimper tore through his bliss, the low sound forcing his beast to focus on their mate, and he carefully withdrew his fangs. He lapped at the wound, treating it gently as he licked up the last few droplets of blood that escaped. Her bear went to work sealing the wound and he gradually lifted his weight from her.

His cock softened as he pulled away, slowly easing from her moist passage until they were no longer connected. With gentle hands he helped her stand and then turned her to rest on the boulder once more.

When their gazes met, he spoke. "You're mine." His touch was soft when he brushed her mating mark. "All mine."

She didn't dispute her claim. Which was good. Because if she did, he'd just do it all over again until she admitted the truth.

She was his.

Just as he was hers.

Chapter Twenty-two

They returned to chaos. Utter, complete chaos.

They'd redressed, his mouth finding her mating mark whenever she turned her attention to redoing her buttons or zipping her shorts. For each piece of clothing she slipped on, he found a way to reach the injury. It was there, on her shoulder and he wanted to order her to walk around in tank tops for the rest of her life. Rain, sun, or snow.

When he'd said that aloud, she'd glared at him and told him he wasn't dictating her wardrobe. He snapped his mouth shut.

He'd just destroy anything that weren't tank tops.

Hours later they eased from the forest, walking hand in hand toward the clan den and the clumps of people milling around the yard.

Evie squeezed his hand, uneasiness pouring from her pores. "Reid?"

He just sighed, staring at each vehicle and then glancing at the newcomers. "Dammit."

"Are we… is the clan in danger?"

"Not unless you're worried about going broke putting money in a swear jar," he mumbled. "Can't I ever get away from these people?"

"Huh?"

They were still a good hundred yards from the clan den and still hadn't been spotted, so he slowed them to a stop and stepped behind her before pointing at the different people. "That one near the back door is the Grayslake Itan, Ty. His curse-hating mate is there chasing after the boy who's chasing the four-year-old who is trying very hard to eat dirt. She decided she was a vegetarian bear last week and dirt, apparently, doesn't have meat.

"The couple snuggling at the other end of the porch are Lauren and Van. Lauren's human and Van's the Enforcer. Then there's Trista and Keen. Last there's Kira and Isaac." He stared around the group, hunting for the other couple who would have driven over. He pointed toward the far wall of the house. It was out of sight of the playing kids and other adults, but not them. "And there, making out like they're fifteen, is my sister and her mate. He took over the Redby pack when I got kicked out."

"They're your family."

"They're my family." There was no denying it. They weren't his by blood, but by heart at least. Damn, he must actually have a heart.

"Why'd you get kicked out?" her voice was soft, not accusing but curious.

"Because they hurt my sister and Kira."

"They didn't know they were your family."

He shrugged. "No one needs to know about connections to treat someone decently. To not scar 'em for no reason. To not torture them."

Evie turned in his arms. "Which is why you're perfect here. You don't care about who these bears are. You care that they're safe. They need that, Reid. I need that."

And he'd give that to her. Even if he had to crack—or cut off—a few heads in the process.

"Uncle Reid!" But first, he had to live through this visit from his family. God, why did he spend the last year making nice with all those dicks?

It's all Clary's fault. Damn acceptance and shit.

When Evie gave his hand a gentle squeeze followed by a soft, reassuring smile, he realized he could conquer anything—kill anyone—as long as he had her at his side.

The End

About the Author

Ex-dance teacher, former accountant and erstwhile collectible doll salesperson, New York Times and USA Today bestselling author Celia Kyle now writes urban fantasy (as Lauren Creed) and paranormal romances for readers who:

1) Like super hunky heroes (they generally get furry)

2) Dig beautiful women (who have a few more curves than the average lady)

3) Love laughing in (and out of) bed.

It goes without saying that there's always a happily-ever-after for her characters, even if there are a few road bumps along the way.

Today she lives in Central Florida and writes full-time with the support of her loving husband and two finicky cats.

If you'd like to be notified of new releases, special sales, and get

FREE eBooks, subscribe here: http://celiakyle.com/news

You can find Celia/Lauren online at:
http://celiakyle.com
http://facebook.com/authorceliakyle
http://twitter.com/celiakyle

CPSIA information can be obtained
at www.ICGtesting.com
Printed in the USA
LVHW092253211219
641379LV00001B/63/P